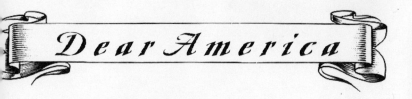

VALLEY OF THE MOON

THE DIARY OF
MARÍA ROSALIA DE MILAGROS

BY SHERRY GARLAND

Scholastic Inc. New York

SONOMA VALLEY,
ALTA CALIFORNIA
1845

October 10, 1845

Tonight I begin my first diary. The Medina family is asleep, and all is quiet throughout the *rancho*. Only the wind racing around the corners of the adobe house and the distant yelp of coyotes break the night silence. I am snuggled in a corner of the kitchen surrounded by baskets of dried corn waiting to be ground. The tile floors feel cold on my bare feet, but I do not mind, for I know no one will find me here.

This diary is mine because the eldest of the Medina daughters, Miguela, tossed it over her balcony into the courtyard. My fingers quickly rescued it from a watery death in the fountain. Señorita Miguela threw it away in a fit of resentment after it was given to her by an American suitor, Señor Henry Johnston. With flashing black eyes she cried out that a girl has no more use for reading and writing than a snake has for gold earrings. She said the diary was an insult to her beauty and charm, then tossed Señor Johnston out, too.

I feel sorry for Señor Johnston, or for any man who has the misfortune of courting headstrong Miguela, but I am not sorry that I now hold her discarded diary in my hands. I must not let anyone see me writing, for I am a servant, a half-Indian orphan, a girl. I am supposed to know nothing but work and obedience. How amazed the Medinas would be if they knew I learned to read and write from a kind old padre at Mission Rafael, many miles from here. Maybe someday I will tell them.

OCTOBER 11

I've been thinking about Padre Ygnacio all day. It was he who found Domingo and me eight years ago beside our dying mother in the rose garden of Mission Rafael near San Francisco Bay. Her body was ravaged with smallpox, and I had placed roses over her face. I think I was about five years old and my brother was about two, but no one knows our ages for sure.

Padre Ygnacio named me María Rosalia - after the Blessed Virgin and because of the roses. He named my brother Domingo because it was a Sunday morning. For a last name he called us Milagros - for it was a miracle indeed that we did not die of the horrible plague that claimed the lives of so many Indians in Alta California. They say that out of forty thousand Suisun people, only two hundred lived. Some smaller tribes lost everyone. How Domingo and I survived is one of the many mysteries of my life.

When Padre Ygnacio found us, we did not speak much Spanish and he did not know our Indian dialect. But of one thing he was sure: Though our mother had the bronze skin of an Indian, our skin was the light brown of *mestizos* - half-Indian and half-Spanish. It was obvious that our father had been a white man. Whether he was a wealthy Spanish landowner, a Spanish soldier from the *presidio* at San Francisco, a Russian fur trapper, or an American merchant sailor, no one knows.

Lupita, the cook, is the closest thing to a mother I have. Her husband, Gregorio, is the head *vaquero* on the ranch. He oversees the men who tend the cattle and horses. It was Gregorio who found me and Domingo at Mission Rafael four years ago and brought us to live at the Medina ranch - Rancho Agua Verde. Lupita and Gregorio have no children of their own but have raised several orphans. I know they care about me, yet my heart feels empty. If I do not know my past, how can I plot my future? I must stop thinking such things and get back to work. If I don't finish grinding this corn, there will be no *tortillas* tomorrow.

Sunday, October 12

I have no place to hide this diary. My room in the servants' quarters is so tiny that I can hardly turn around. I share it with Ramona, the seamstress. We sleep on woven straw pallets on the floor and roll them up each morning. We take turns sitting on the one chair at the one tiny table. Whoever doesn't get the chair sits on an overturned wooden bucket. The adobe walls and ceiling are stained with black soot from the fireplace and tallow candles.

But our quarters are not as bleak as some. Ramona saves scraps of cloth from the sewing projects. Our walls are alive with color - a wool tapestry, one finely embroidered hanging that depicts the Holy Virgin, and another hanging that shimmers with flowers. Even our floor has a wool rug made of remnants from the spring sheepshearing. Pegs line the walls for our sparse clothing. Baskets hang from the heavy timber beams for food and miscellaneous items. It is better than the room I shared with four other orphans at Mission Rafael.

OCTOBER 13

The Medina daughters saw me in the courtyard today carrying the diary. Miguela was amused and said I could keep it. "Perhaps you might use it for fire kindling, Rosa," she said with a toss of her black curls. Miguela is seventeen and has been available for marriage for two years. She is a great beauty but has ignored all the men who call on her and has refused several proposals. If I were rich, I would pay a man every *peso* I owned to take her away from this ranch.

Rafaela, the middle daughter, who is aged fifteen, is gentle and sweet but very sickly. She coughs often, and her skin is paler than white lilies. She told Miguela not to be so unkind because I am more like family than a servant. Bless her soul, how I wish her words were true.

Gabriela, who is eleven and like a little sister to me, said to just ignore Miguela. Everyone knows how Miguela is, but still her words stung.

OCTOBER 14

I am in the goat pen seizing a moment to write in my diary. I milked the goats faster than lightning so that I might have a free moment. I carry the diary with me all the time, tied to my waist with a sash and hidden under my skirt. I dare not write at night in my room, for Ramona is a light sleeper.

I have no ink, so I am using beet juice. It leaves an uneven pale red color, but it must do until I find real ink. For a pen, I am using a sharpened black feather from the tail of Paladin, Señor Medina's favorite fighting rooster. Domingo stole the feather from the chicken coop and gave it to me. All I think of while doing chores is the moment I will open this diary and write. It is my island of refuge in a sea of work.

OCTOBER 15

Señor Johnston is here again. I like him very much. He speaks to me kindly and does not order me around. He owns a merchant business in the small town of Yerba Buena on San Francisco Bay south of here. Being twenty-eight years of age and settled, he is now looking for a wife. He has decided upon Señorita Miguela (may Heaven help him!) and has visited Rancho Agua Verde many times this year.

Señor Johnston is waiting for his brother and family, who are coming by wagon train from Missouri to join him in California. They will arrive first at Sutter's Fort in the Sacramento Valley, where Johnston will go to meet them. A few years ago there were very few foreigners in Alta California, just some sailors and fur trappers. Now they come in a steady stream - mostly farmers from Missouri. There are hundreds of them, especially in the Sacramento Valley northeast of here.

Lupita does not trust the *norteamericanos*. She says they are supposed to become loyal Mexican citizens, learn to speak Spanish, and become Catholics in exchange for land. But not all of them do as they agreed. She especially dislikes the foreigner Johann Sutter, who encourages other foreigners to come to California illegally without permission from the Mexican government. There are already squatters on Señor Medina's lands. Lupita thinks they will take over Alta California before long.

I do not care what Lupita says. I like Señor Johnston, even if he is an *americano*. He is beside himself with excitement about his brother's arrival. But he is worried. The snows will soon start to fall on top of the Sierra Nevada mountains to the east, causing deep drifts and icy rocks that make the passes treacherous to cross. If the Johnston family does not clear the mountains by the end of this month, they are surely doomed.

October 16

Spent a pleasant morning working in the courtyard that is surrounded by the thick walls of the *casa grande* on four sides. I wonder if the Medina house will ever be completed. Every year, the Indian workers add a bit more. When the main house was first built, it was a simple, one-story structure like nearly all the *ranchos* in northern Alta California. But after Señora Medina and Miguela saw the grand *rancho* that General Vallejo was building at Petaluma a few miles away, they insisted on having a second story with balconies and rambling rose vines. At the moment, only the Medina family has upstairs bedrooms with balconies. Everyone else, servants and guests alike, sleeps downstairs. I do not mind for walking up and down stairs makes my legs ache.

Drew ten buckets of water from the well to tend the herbs, beans, squash, pumpkins, melons, onions, and hot chiles in the garden near the kitchen door. Swept the veranda that is roofed with brown clay tiles. Pruned the rambling Castilian roses that climb up the posts to the upstairs bedroom balconies. Picked late maturing pears from Señor Medina's cherished fruit trees. I am tired, but am writing during *siesta* while everyone else rests. Writing brings me more joy than sleep! Nothing would make me happier than to write all day and all night.

OCTOBER 17

¡Madre mía! My secret is uncovered! While I was in the courtyard writing in my diary today, Señor Johnston appeared out of nowhere. I was afraid he would be angry that I had it, but his large blue eyes grew wide like an owl's. He said to me in his best Spanish (which I am sorry to say is not very good): "Rosalia! I cannot believe you are writing! How did you learn such skills?"

I begged Johnston not to tell anyone, for it would only mean trouble for me. I explained how Padre Ygnacio taught the Indian boys at Mission Rafael to read and write. He let me sit quietly at the back of the room and I helped Domingo, who detested lessons and being indoors. The California missions were closing down, anyway, and the padre did not care if the rules said girls did not need an education. He said if a girl wanted to read and write, he would not stop her. He was very generous and tolerant when it came to the mission *indios*.

Johnston was so astonished that he dug into his leather saddlebag and handed me a bottle of ink, a very nice brass point, and two turkey quills. Now the ink flows onto the pages almost as fast as I think of words.

October 18

Señor Johnston is very impatient to hear from his brother. He says his niece, Nelly, is thirteen, and he hopes that she and I will become friends. Johnston is teaching me English so that I will be able to keep Nelly company.

This morning Señor Medina invited Johnston to accompany him and Gregorio to inspect the *rancho*. Señor Medina rides every day except Sunday from one grazing field to another checking on the vast herds of cattle, horses, fighting bulls, sheep, goats, pigs, and fields of wheat, barley, and corn.

Miguela rode along with them, dressed in a short *bolero* jacket, baggy pantaloons, and a perky black hat with silver disks. She is an accomplished horsewoman who rides like a man when it suits her fancy, straddling the horse instead of sitting sidesaddle like a lady. She can throw a *lazo* with great skill.

Señor Johnston says I am the only one who is willing to explain Mexican customs to him. He is very frustrated with Miguela. I told him he must stand under her balcony singing and reciting poetry. I tore a page out of my diary and wrote down the words to a passionate song that is famous among all the Spanish women. Johnston paid Tomás, an Indian house servant, to strum a guitar. Johnston has a clear, fine voice but he destroyed the rhythm and flow of the language. Miguela only laughed and closed the shutters. I think Señor Johnston is blinded by her beauty. Poor Johnston.

SUNDAY, OCTOBER 19

We got up before dawn to make the long trip into Sonoma for Sunday mass. Afterward we went to the house of Señora Medina's widowed sister, Gertruda, who lives with her ancient mother-in-law and four children. I love visiting their little adobe house that faces the plaza. On the north side of the plaza, next to the barracks, is the house of General Mariano Vallejo, the wealthiest man in northern California and the most powerful. It was he who founded Sonoma and laid out the plaza. He also built the barracks and pays the soldiers out of his own pocket because the government of Mexico refuses to send aid to Alta California, her most distant province. Vallejo's grand *rancho* is at Petaluma, east of here, but General Vallejo spends most of his time here in Sonoma in a house not so grand.

LATER

Horrible, horrible news! After the meal, a messenger pounded at the door. Señor Johnston's brother, wife, and their two youngest children were killed in an awful accident while crossing the Sierras. Their oxen slipped near a cliff, and while trying to upright the wagon, the parents and children plunged to their deaths. Only Nelly and an older brother survived.

Poor Johnston was inconsolable. He wept openly, then said he must go immediately to Sutter's Fort to get his nephew and niece. He asked Señor Medina if I could accompany him, thinking it might be a comfort to his niece to have a companion her own age in this sad time and because I am an orphan, too. Señor Medina quickly consented and is sending along supplies, extra horses, and an Indian guide to show Johnston the quickest route to Sutter's Fort.

I must close for now; the horses are packed and ready.

OCTOBER 21

We have been pushing the horses hard for over two days. We awake before dawn and travel even after dark. We are passing through the most beautiful country — pleasant hills and valleys lush with autumn wildflowers, pine trees, live oaks, and *manzanita* shrubs. Occasionally we pass shepherds bringing their herds down from the mountains for winter grazing. The air is crisp and reminds me that light snows are already falling on top of the distant Sierras. I can only imagine the misery of the American settlers who have the misfortune of not getting across before winter sets in.

We changed horses at a small, bleak *rancho* and set out again. I have never been so far from home. It is frightening, yet exciting. I only wish we did not travel at such a pace. My bottom is so saddle sore, I may never walk again.

October 22

Señor Johnston is resting a moment. We are on a hillock and I can see Sutter's Fort below beside a slough that runs to the Sacramento River. The fort is a large rectangular building with a tall armed bastion at each end, where guards watch for hostile Indians — those who never lived at the missions or became part of *californio* society like Lupita and Gregorio. Though their numbers are greatly reduced, some of these unfriendly Indians still raid *ranchos* for livestock and cause great havoc. I am grateful that they are not as fierce as the tribes of the Great Plains that Señor Johnston told me about. Though I am part Indian myself, I am as much afraid of hostile Indian attacks as any *anglo* girl.

From the top of each bastion roof flies a flag. The adobe walls are several feet thick and contain few windows. Johann Sutter hails from a far-off country called Switzerland, so he named his settlement New Helvetia, the Latin word for Switzerland. Everyone else calls it Sutter's Fort or simply Sacramento, after the nearest river.

Near the fort is a corral for livestock, and in the distance fields of grain are being harvested. I can clearly see the Indian laborers loading big *carretas* pulled by oxen. Fur, cattle hides, tallow, and handicrafts are being loaded onto barges at the slough. The barges will carry the goods down the river all the way to San Francisco Bay to waiting merchant ships. The ships, many of them American, will haul the goods around the tip of South America to the United States.

It is almost dark, and I hear bells from the fort signaling the laborers to stop work and return to their quarters. I see smoke rising from chimneys and I can smell bread baking. Johnston is ready to ride again, so I must close for now.

Later that Night

It is dark now, and I am in a room set aside for arriving emigrants. Nelly Johnston is sound asleep. She had not slept well for a week because of grief and has finally cried herself out. She is a very quiet girl, thin from nearly starving on the long trip from Missouri. Her wavy hair is the color of an oak leaf turning bronze, and she has a few freckles on her nose.

Nelly does not speak a word of Spanish, but through Johnston and with the little English I know, she communicated her feelings. She is still in shock because she traveled so far, so long, through such hardships, only to lose her parents on the final leg of the journey. Not to hostile Indians when they crossed the Great Plains, or to thirst, or to disease or hunger, or to vicious animals, but to a stupid mishap, to the slipping of an ox's hoof. Her brother, Walter, is a fine-looking young man of sixteen, with the same bright blue eyes of Señor Johnston. He blames himself for the accident, though Nelly assures everyone that Walter could not have stopped the oxen, no matter how strong he was.

Señor Sutter is most generous. He is a slightly stocky man, with a balding head, a large, droopy mustache, and a tiny tuft of beard on his chin. He speaks with a heavy German accent. He said the Johnston children may stay as long as needed. He will provide them with employment, if they choose. They will decide tomorrow. Tonight everyone is drained, I from the long ride, they from the emotional reunion and grief.

OCTOBER 23

I rose early, while Nelly slept, to explore Sutter's Fort. The aroma of fresh bread baking in the beehive-shaped *horno* filled the air. Not far from the oven, women were busy in the weaving room, working at the spinning wheel and loom making cloth and rugs. Near them, the cooper assembled wooden barrels and hammered metal hoops around them.

At the center of the fort, Señor Sutter sat in his office giving instructions to Indian laborers and scribbling in his ledgers. Nearby the blacksmith's hammer clanged against an anvil. His bellows sighed and hissed as his assistant fanned the flames, sending a wave of warmth into the chilly morning air. To one side of the blacksmith was the carpenter's shop, where a sawyer cut and sawed boards for furniture and buildings, and to the other side was the granary filled high with wheat, barley, and corn. In the kitchen women ground corn, churned butter, and cooked pots of stew.

Outside, at the trappers' station, burly men dressed in buckskin were piling furs of beaver, otter, bear, and deer for trade with the merchant ships. I wanted to stay longer, but after an early breakfast, Señor Johnston loaded what few belongings his nephew and niece had onto the extra horse and we left.

OCTOBER 24

Rode all day. Nelly got scared when we passed a party of Suisun Indian men leading a string of horses to trade at Sutter's Fort. She said her greatest fear while crossing the plains in the covered wagon was Indian attacks. Señor Johnston assured Nelly that the Indians were peaceful. Nelly was very surprised to find out I was half-Indian. "I thought you were Mexican," she said. Her words got me to thinking. Just when did I stop being an Indian and start becoming a Mexican? Was it when I learned to speak

Spanish? Or when I became a Christian and celebrated Christian holidays? Or when I dressed in Spanish clothes and ate Spanish foods? Did all those outer trappings change who I was on the inside? I couldn't figure it out myself, so I dropped the subject.

OCTOBER 25

We arrived back at the Medina *rancho* around dusk. Nelly is sharing a room with Gabriela. I do not think Nelly wanted to do so, but she had no choice. Señora Medina would never allow a guest to stay in the servants' quarters where I live. I feel sorry for Nelly. Each time I see her sad eyes, I cannot help but remember the pain and loneliness I felt when my own mother died. It is a pain that never goes away.

Nelly acts uncomfortable around the Medina daughters. I think I know what she is feeling. The Medinas are *criollos*, from the highest class of society in Alta California, being descendants of pure Spanish blood, as their white skin indicates. They disdain work and consider it beneath them to participate in any manual chores. Their lives center around social gatherings and attending church. Nelly is from common stock and is used to working hard. She knows how to cook and sew; she knows how to make soap and bake bread. She wears sturdy, plain clothing and does not care if her hair has fancy ribbons. She is more comfortable in my company or with Lupita in the kitchen.

This evening, Nelly said she feels like a burden and asked if she might help with the chores. Señora Medina assured Nelly that, as a guest, she is not expected to lift a finger. Nelly looked so disappointed, I snuck her into the kitchen and let her make something called "corn bread." It is made of cornmeal similar to *tortillas*, but she added eggs and oil to make a batter and baked it in a pan like a cake. She served it at the late evening meal. Señor Johnston slathered his piece with butter, then proclaimed it was the best he'd ever eaten. The Medinas politely nibbled at it and paid compliments, but I know they did not care for it.

Walter Johnston is quiet and moody. He stayed at the corrals watching the *vaqueros* perform roping feats. Walter's blue eyes are so sad and beautiful. Oh, how I wish we could speak each other's language better!

Sunday, October 26

I stayed home from church today because Rafaela was sick. She was born very small, and all her life she has had spells of weakness. The slightest fever or cold often turns into serious illness. So at the first sign of any sickness, she takes to her bed. While Rafaela slept, I told Nelly about my diary. I was amazed to learn that she barely knows how to write her own name. She said she was too busy with chores back in Missouri to go to school.

October 27

Señor Johnston and Walter left for Yerba Buena on urgent business early this morning. Nelly is staying until Johnston sends for her. I think Nelly was relieved. She is learning some Spanish, and I am learning more English. We made a game of it while I watered the plants in the courtyard this morning. Nelly tried sitting for a while, embroidering with Rafaela, but grew restless. She tried riding with Miguela, but was frightened of the high-spirited horse. Gabriela watched us doing chores but drew the line at doing any work herself. She tried to get Nelly to play doll games, but Nelly politely declined. Gabriela and I used to be playmates, but as we grew older her mother put a stop to it. I love Gabriela like a little sister, but I know in her eyes we can never be equals. I think Señora Medina has finally given up on making Nelly sit about and do nothing.

October 28

I saw Señora Medina alone in the family *sala* saying prayers in front of the wooden altar. As always, she wore layers of dark, somber clothing, rosary beads, and a heavy silver cross encrusted with jewels. Her black hair was pulled straight back from her forehead and twisted behind her head, pinned with a tortoise-shell comb. She is so graceful and refined.

I mustered the courage to ask her if Domingo and I could travel to Mission Rafael on the occasion of *El Día de los Muertos* — the Day of the Dead — which will be celebrated in four days. People all over Mexico pay honor to their departed loved ones by visiting their gravesides.

Señora Medina looked at the crucifix above the

altar and quickly made the sign of the cross. I knew she was thinking about her own four little boys who all died as infants. Only her three daughters survived. Lupita says it is because they were named after the archangels.

Señora Medina said she would consider my request, then she told me to ask God for guidance. "Remember, *Dios provida* — God will provide." That is Señora Medina's favorite saying.

I knelt beside the altar and prayed with all my heart that somehow Domingo and I could return for just one day to see our mother's grave. I wanted to pray that God would somehow reveal to us who our mother and father were, but I decided that I should not burden God with more than one miracle at a time.

OCTOBER 29

My heart is heavy. Señor Johnston has sent word for Nelly to join him in Yerba Buena. I have never had such a wonderful companion. At the news Nelly ran outside and climbed a live oak tree. I followed and sat beside her. She was clinging to a small gold locket that never leaves her neck. It belonged to her mother and is her most prized possession.

Lupita tells me it's good to cry once in a while and talk about feelings, so I urged Nelly to tell me why she was so sad. She told me it seemed like everyone she cares about leaves her. I assured her we would still be friends and see each other, especially if Miguela marries her uncle. The Medinas love to visit relatives.

She sniffed, then laughed. "I reckon we'll have to play matchmakers and make sure they marry." We made a secret vow to each other to do our best.

OCTOBER 30

Nelly, Ramona, and I spent the morning gathering pumpkins and squash. We have a fine crop this year. My hands are cramped from cutting open pumpkins and scooping out the insides. I spread the seeds in the warm sun. We will have many *pepitas* for recipes this winter.

We accidentally left the garden gate unlatched, and while our backs were turned a mule got into the melons. Big slobbers drooled from his lips as he chewed the rinds. Flowers got caught on his ears and formed a hat. I tried to be angry, but the sight was so hilarious that we all broke into laughter.

LATER

Gabriela did a spiteful thing after *siesta*. She told Nelly that she should not be playing with a common servant and insisted they play with dolls. I know Nelly was disappointed, but she feels obligated to the Medinas for their hospitality. Tears stung my eyes when Gabriela pushed me aside and took Nelly by the hand. It still hurts to think about it.

Señora Medina finally consented to allow Domingo and me to travel to Mission Rafael to visit our mother's grave. She only did so because Gregorio will be taking Nelly to Señor Johnston's house in Yerba Buena, which is across San Francisco Bay from Mission Rafael.

OCTOBER 31

Tonight at midnight begins the celebration of *El Día de los Muertos* — the Day of the Dead. Everyone throughout Mexico will honor their departed loved ones, starting with the dead children, *los angelitos*, the first night.

All morning I helped Lupita prepare *tamales* and special treats. We made the finely ground corn into *masa* dough and spread it onto dried corn husks, then added shredded hog meat and spices. We folded them into neat little bundles before sliding them into the pot to steam. Ramona, who is the first orphan that Lupita took under her wing, was in charge of watching the *horno*. In it baked the loaves of *pan de los muertos* shaped like skulls, or loaves with crossbones on top. I patted out thin *tortillas* and thicker *gorditas* until my hands and arms ached, then dripped sweat for hours cooking them on the hot *comal*.

Señora Medina decorated the family altar with marigolds, candles, crosses, and draped black cloth around the ancestral oil portraits hanging in the main corridor. I do not like the way their dark eyes follow me when I pass by. Sometimes the faces enter my dreams, especially the handsome face of Señor Medina's younger brother who died tragically young.

Señora Medina laid out four pieces of lacy infant clothing from the four Medina babies who died. She dabbed at her eyes as she placed toys around the altar.

It has been nine years since her last son died, but she still grieves.

After lunch, Lupita sent me to the courtyard garden to gather more marigolds for the altar. All the Medina daughters were there, dressed in layers of black ruffled petticoats and lacy black *mantillas*. Señor Medina suddenly walked into the garden, and the girls rushed to him. He has been in Monterey, and everyone missed him sorely. As the girls each bowed and kissed his hand, he said sweet words and handed them pretty ribbons. I watched from the shadows, my heart aching for a father's love.

Gabriela saw me and said, "Papá, may I give Rosa one of my red ribbons?" His eyes glowed with pride as he nodded, but it made me feel awful, for if there is one thing I do not want it is pity.

November 1

All Saints' Day. Blessed be the name of all the saints in Heaven. Amen. While it was still dark outside, I packed food for the trip to Mission Rafael. I put on my finest embroidered skirt and white blouse. Lupita wove my hair into a long black braid and tied it with the new red ribbon. Around my shoulder I slung my striped wool *rebozo* woven by the *rancho* Indians. We left before dawn, with Domingo still sleepy eyed and grumbling.

Nelly and I were sullen, knowing it might be the last time we saw each other for who knows how long. We arrived at Mission Rafael at dusk. Gregorio left me and Domingo at the mission while he took Nelly on to Johnston's home in Yerba Buena. I said a tearful good-bye to Nelly as she climbed into a boat to be ferried across the cold waters of San Francisco Bay.

Like all the churches throughout Mexico, the Mission Rafael chapel was draped in black cloth and decorated with signs of death and mortality — skulls, crossbones, skeletons, coffins. We joined a procession of locals singing and carrying candles, food, and flowers as they walked slowly to the *campo santo*, where their loved ones are buried. Mass was celebrated at the cemetery gate. I looked for Padre Ygnacio, but did not see his gray hair and inquisitive face.

After mass, people moved over the grounds to the graves of their departed ones, marked mostly with wooden crosses. Our mother's grave has no cross. I found it only because it is near an oak tree and five years ago I planted a rosebush there. Most of the Indians who died in the smallpox epidemic were buried in massive pits or burned in funeral pyres.

I scattered marigolds over the grave, and Domingo lit candles. After praying for our mother's soul, I spread a blanket on the ground and set up the food and drink. As usual, Domingo wanted to hear about our mother and our early days at the mission. I told him what I remembered: our mother's voice, the little song she sang to him as she rocked him in her arms, and the ever-present smell of tangy herbs on her fingers. It was not much, but Domingo grew quiet. He pulled his *sarape* closer and hugged his arms.

SUNDAY, NOVEMBER 2

All Souls' Day. We held vigil all last night over our mother's grave. I wish I knew what foods my mother liked, but I do not even know what her name was. I hummed the tune and held Domingo tight, for he was shivering like a lost lamb. I did not close my eyes until the early hours of the morning, when the candles had burned down. I saw no apparitions, but I felt a warm presence after midnight. Maybe it was my mother's spirit, maybe the warmth from the candle flames.

The old mission looks so abandoned. Its stucco walls and bright orange tiled roof are in shambles. The tiny room where I spent many happy days has birds' nests in its chimney. I have learned that Padre Ygnacio left shortly after we did. With him went all hope of learning who my parents were.

NOVEMBER 3

Early this morning Gregorio took us to Señor Johnston's home in Yerba Buena across the bay, then he left to oversee the transfer of hides and tallow from the *rancho*. Though it has been but one day since we parted, Nelly and I hugged like long-lost sisters. Johnston's house is small and bleak and lacks a woman's touch. I cannot in a thousand years imagine Señorita Miguela wanting to live here. But the supply store is large and fine. The shelves are lined with products imported from Mexico, South America, Asia, Europe, and the United States. I told Señor Johnston that he should bring Miguela here to see the store. That will win her heart faster than a pretty bouquet.

Yerba Buena is a dismal little place with only a handful of adobe houses and a few businesses, mostly those related to shipping and trading. But the view of the bay is breathtaking, especially when a gentle fog hovers over the water. I can clearly see the strait leading into the mouth of the bay. It reminds me of a golden gate when the setting sun hits it.

Two ships are docked in the bay. They are being loaded with goods from local *ranchos*. For miles on end, huge oxen-drawn two-wheeled *carretas* or long mule trains travel from Sonoma Valley, Napa Valley, and other nearby regions with their loads — hides, tallow, and wool products such as blankets and rugs woven by Indian servants. Some of the goods come down rivers on barges. The smell of leather and fat permeates the air around the bay. It is unpleasant, but Señor Johnston says it is the smell of money.

NOVEMBER 4

Fog rolled in last night and did not lift all day. I had forgotten how cold and damp the weather here can be. Domingo, Nelly, and I walked up and down the muddy streets and saw all there was to see in an hour's time. Besides Yerba Buena there is also Mission Dolores and the nearby *Presidio de San Francisco* garrisoned with a few soldiers and their families. Johnston says the population of Yerba Buena altogether, not including the Indians, is about two hundred. Every time I see a white man, be he foreigner or Spanish *ranchero* or soldier, I cannot help but wonder if he is my father.

I am chilled to the bone and cannot wait to return to Rancho Agua Verde. They call it that because there is an underground spring that forms a green pool of bubbly hot water on the property. I wish I were in the warm water now!

NOVEMBER 5

Nelly and I washed Johnston's clothes, changed his bedding, swept his floors, removed cobwebs and three years of dust. I put flowers in a gourd on the table. It was out of boredom more than anything else that we did the work, but Johnston was moved to tears to see the place so freshened. I asked Johnston why he wanted to marry Miguela, who is so hot-tempered and headstrong, who rides a horse like a man and can rope a cow as well as any young *vaquero*, while the middle daughter, Rafaela, is gentle and refined.

Johnston agreed that Rafaela is indeed lovely and sweet, but she is weak and sickly. He thinks she will most likely not be able to bear even one child. Miguela, on the other hand, has hips and thighs as strong as the trunks of an oak tree. "I wager she will produce fifteen children," he said. I wonder what Miguela would do if she knew he only cared for her because of her hips and thighs. I am still laughing.

NOVEMBER 6

It is raining, and Domingo is running and whooping again. He refuses to obey me and spends his days in the street playing games with the sons of the *presidio* soldiers. He has decided he wants to be a soldier. Before now it was a *vaquero*, and before that a bull-fighter. Tomorrow, who knows?

Señor Johnston said that we could select a gift from his store. I made my decision in less than a heartbeat. I chose a block of hard ink. Now I am set to write in my diary for many, many days.

NOVEMBER 7

Saw whales plowing the water, blowing geysers out of their spouts. They are such magnificent creatures. We borrowed Johnston's spyglass for a closer look. Nelly had never seen a whale and could not be calmed down.

NOVEMBER 8

Gregorio arrived with wagons piled high with cowhides and pack mules weighed down with tallow. You never heard such laughing and shouting when the *vaqueros* finished their work. They headed for the *cantinas*, and their celebrating is still going on. I can hear the lively guitars and the clack of castanets from down the street as the men and women dance the lively *fandango*.

Nelly and I slipped down to a *cantina* and peeked inside. The dancing girls were lovely with their flashing black eyes, and their long hair that flew around them as they twirled. One wore red petticoats! The music started slow but grew faster until the girl spun in a frenzy. She shouted and clicked the castanets.

Her expression grew fierce as she slapped her skirt and stomped her feet like she was trying to kill spiders.

NOVEMBER 11

We left before dawn today. I hated to leave Nelly, but my heart is homesick for Rancho Agua Verde. The carts are now filled with American cloth, sugar, flour, dry goods, tools, and furniture for the Medinas' *casa grande*.

By dark, we reached the Sonoma hills and looked down at the beautiful valley. Gregorio says that Sonoma is the Indian word that means "valley of the moon." We are spending the night near a creek. The *vaqueros* unsaddled their horses and rolled out their blankets in front of campfires. One is playing his *guitarra*, and another is singing a song of lost love. The music is lovely, and the stars are breathtaking. I can see the house of General Vallejo below lit up with candles. Across the stillness I hear the laughter of his children and the clink of china. I am so glad to be back in my valley of the moon.

November 12

Passed through Sonoma at daybreak. Gregorio stopped at Gertruda's house to give her some china dishes she had ordered months ago. She gave me and Domingo a sweet *buñuelo* and a cup of hot chocolate.

Five miles from the *rancho* we passed the *calaveras*, the place where cows are slaughtered, their hides skinned off, and tallow made from their fat. It is an unpleasant, reeking place, covered with cattle bones bleached white by the sun. Domingo wanted to bring a skull home, but Gregorio made him put it back.

November 15

Too busy to write. The chores piled up while I was gone. Lupita strained her back and has not been able to cook or do housework. Ramona tried to do the cooking, but is a poor substitute. No time for anything but work.

November 17

For days, the Medina daughters have acted like silly geese, squealing and fighting over the new cloth, jewelry, and trinkets. Miguela is the loudest of all, her voice carrying out the windows to the courtyard. When Rafaela, soft-spoken and timid, does not get what she wants, she slips into a corner and sulks. Only Gabriela uses common sense, but she does not often win over Rafaela. I miss Nelly so much!

November 18

Today the sisters were in the *gran sala* engaged in a loud argument over a piece of beautiful Asian blue silk brocade, when we heard Señor Medina's boots clicking on the corridor floor. He walked in and glared at them. As usual, he had been riding the *rancho* examining his livestock. He wore a short jacket, a red waist sash, a broad-rimmed black hat trimmed in silver, a *sarape*, and boots with heavy iron spurs. Though forty years old, he still sits tall in the saddle and is as handsome as any man in California. His small mustache twitched, and his face hardened. The fighting stopped instantly, and the girls scrambled to line up, curtsy, and kiss his hand. But Rafaela's face, normally pale as a ghost, was red, and he knew they had been fighting. In disgust, he turned to me and said, "Well, Rosa, what are they fighting over this time?"

My face grew hot. If I told the truth, the girls would hate me. If I lied to Señor Medina, I would feel like a traitor. I shrugged and feigned ignorance.

The señor saw the brocade on the floor and picked it up. He turned to his daughters, who dropped their gaze in embarrassment. He then pushed the finely woven cloth into my arms.

"It looks to me like Rosalia is the only girl in this house who knows how to act like a young lady, so this silk will go to her." He twirled and walked out, his spurs spinning and jingling. Words cannot convey the sear of hatred I felt aimed at me from Miguela's black eyes. Rafaela merely sighed and shrugged her shoulders. Gabriela laughed and said she would help me design a pretty dress. She looped her arm through mine and we sought out Ramona.

November 22

Lupita is finally well enough to work again, so I have more time to write. Ramona finished my dress tonight. It is one of the finest dresses in all of Alta California. Who would believe that it belongs to me, a motherless servant, who has no more need of a fine dress than a snake has need of a pair of gold earrings, as Miguela once so aptly observed.

Sunday, November 23

Today is the Feast of Christ the King. I wore my new dress to mass at the church in Sonoma. Señora Medina seemed pleased that I had a new dress. Miguela, as usual, cast spears of anger at me. Señor Medina saw me at breakfast and smiled. He put his strong hand under my chin and turned my face so that the morning sun landed squarely in my eyes. *"Muy bonita,"* is all he said, and nodded.

The mass was fine, and the singing stirred my soul. It seemed that all eyes stared at my beautiful dress, and my heart swelled with pride and vanity. After mass, I saw Miguela talking to Pedro, an Indian boy who works in the blacksmith's stables, a raggedy, skinny boy who reeks of manure. I was walking toward the cart, admiring the dresses and fine suits of the Vallejo family several yards ahead of me when suddenly I felt a hard blow to my back that knocked me into a puddle of mud flavored with a pile of fresh horse manure. When I rose up, I was covered with filth from head to toe. I saw Pedro running away, then heard Miguela shrieking with laughter. Hot tears burned my cheeks as I ran back to the mission chapel, passing directly in front of the Medina daughters. Miguela demanded to know where I was going.

I paused at the stone steps and swallowed hard. "I am going to ask Our Heavenly Father to forgive you," I said. This time it was Gabriela I heard laughing. She followed me inside, and we prayed together. Afterward we went to the horse trough, and she helped me wash off the mud as best as possible. When I asked her why Miguela hated me so much, Gabriela just shrugged.

"Miguela hates everyone. Just ignore her. If we are fortunate, she'll be married and move within the year. Won't that be wonderful?"

Wonderful, indeed. But poor Señor Johnston. He does not deserve such a shrew, even if she has the strongest thighs and hips in all of California.

November 25

I am furious at the lead nanny goat, Arabella! Today while I milked the goats, I laid my diary down on top of a fence rail. When I turned around, Arabella had it in her mouth, merrily chewing on the pages. Now my precious diary is tattered and ugly. I will never forgive that goat!

November 29

I have avoided Miguela all week. The less I see of her, the better. This morning the family received an invitation from Señor Johnston to visit him in Yerba Buena. Perhaps he is taking my advice and will show Miguela his fine store. Gabriela asked if I might come along as her personal servant, but I feigned illness. Though I do love traveling of any kind, the thought of riding in the same wagon as Miguela makes me ill indeed.

Sunday, November 30

The household is quiet and peaceful with the feuding sisters gone. Lupita has given me the entire day off, thinking that I am really sick. I am taking advantage of my freedom by slipping books from Señor Medina's library. Though a cold wind blows and rain patters upon the roof tiles, I am snuggled warm in my tiny room beside a fire. A finer day I have never experienced.

December 3

I am doomed! This morning, Señor Villareal, the *mayordomo* who is responsible for managing the business affairs of Rancho Agua Verde, came into Señor Medina's library unexpectedly. The grim little man saw me poring over a book of poetry written by a famous Spanish nun. Señor Villareal said nothing, but I know he is troubled. He is probably waiting for the family to return before he dispenses punishment. I cannot sleep for worry.

DECEMBER 4

¡Gracias a Dios! Miguela has consented to marry Señor Henry Johnston. Two days ago Johnston gave the letter of proposal to Señor Medina, who presented it to his daughter. When she said yes, the men lit up cigars and shook hands. I wish I had been there to see.

The wedding is to take place in January, a practical time of the year, for the *rancho* is not so consumed with work. Miguela is to move to Yerba Buena. I am so happy, I can hardly stand still. The *mayordomo* apparently said nothing to Señor Medina about catching me reading. I hide whenever I see his grim face.

DECEMBER 5

Miguela spent the morning with Ramona designing her wedding trousseau. The gown is to be of white silk, with hundreds of tiny seed pearls on the bodice, stiff ruffles on the neck, and fine French lace on the cuffs. Señor Johnston has gone to Monterey, the capital city of Alta California, to purchase the materials. Ramona said that I am to help with the sewing, for I am cursed with having a good eye for tiny stitches. Miguela is all thumbs when it comes to needlework. She prefers to ride her horse over the windy hills. I wonder how she will ever adjust to being a merchant's wife.

SUNDAY, DECEMBER 7

After mass I cornered Pedro and asked him why he had pushed me in the mud that day. Though Pedro is strong, my knee kept him pinned to the adobe wall. He finally broke down and confessed that Miguela had given him a small loaf of *pan dulce* for doing it. He said he had not eaten bread in months. I looked into his dirty face and at his skinny ribs and suddenly was moved with compassion for this wretched boy. He is an orphaned Indian like myself, and is no more than a slave for the blacksmith who never gives him enough to eat. I let him go without taking retribution. Hunger makes a person do awful things sometimes. Perhaps I would have done the same. I returned to the chapel and prayed for forgiveness for my wicked thoughts.

December 8

General Vallejo was kind enough to send Señor Medina some old newspapers that had arrived from Mexico City last week. Señor Medina spent the day with his head buried in the crumpled, yellowed papers. He smoked one cigar after another, grumbling, and complaining about what he read, rising occasionally to pace the floor and wave his hands.

Alta California is Mexico's farthest removed province, and news takes months, even a year to arrive here, especially the far-removed north. Californians did not find out about Mexico's independence from Spain until 1822 — almost a year after the fact. We are never aware of what is happening with the government of Mexico, nor do we know who is president nor what laws are being changed. That is why Spanish families in Alta California do not call themselves Mexicans, but *californios*. Mexico City cannot adequately rule from so remote a distance, so in the eyes of most *californios*, we might as well be an independent country.

After reading the papers, Señor Medina ordered his favorite horse saddled and took off toward Sonoma in a greatly agitated state. The daughters gathered around their mother, twisting their hands, asking what was wrong.

Señora Medina calmed them with her soothing voice. "It is some political debate. Something about the former province of Texas. It is nothing for us to be concerned about." Then she led them into the family *sala* to pray.

In the kitchen, Gregorio told me that Señor Medina is worried that Texas is going to join the United States. Doing so will surely mean war between Mexico and the United States because Mexico never relinquished claim on Texas ten years ago when the Texans declared independence.

I hope that California will not be involved in this war. Surely we are too far removed for the *americanos* to send their army. Gregorio says that if anyone fights here, it will be American settlers at Sutter's Fort or merchants along San Francisco Bay — people like Henry Johnston and Nelly.

My heart is sick at the thought of going to war against Nelly's family. She is my dear friend. No matter what happens, I cannot think of her as the enemy.

❧❧❧

DECEMBER 10

Miguela is quiet today. Señor Johnston has not returned from Monterey yet with the materials for the wedding gown. I wonder if Miguela is worried about Señor Johnston or about her wedding silk.

DECEMBER 12

Today is the Fiesta of the Virgin of Guadalupe. I was awakened by the sound of drums, cymbals, and rattling gourds outside my window. I saw a long, solemn procession of Suisun Indians, led by Chief Solano, on their way to Sonoma Mission, which has been decorated with roses and colored paper. Men were dressed in their finest feathers and jingling necklaces and anklets of seashells or bits of colored rocks. Women wore colorful clothing with fine embroidery and many-colored *rebozos* wrapped around their shoulders. At the head of the procession was a painted wooden image of the Holy Virgin of Guadalupe, her dark skin glistening in the morning sunlight.

Señor Medina gave all the servants the day off, and we joined in the procession. The Indians believe that the Blessed Virgin María appeared three hundred years ago to an Indian peasant, Juan Diego, near the town of Guadalupe. She instructed Juan Diego to tell the bishop to build a church on a nearby hill. To convince the doubting bishop, she made roses grow where only cactus lived, and her image was miraculously emblazoned on Diego's cloak. But most importantly, the Virgin who appeared to him was not the light-skinned woman depicted in Spanish paintings, but a woman of dark skin like that of the Indians.

After the mass, people sat under trees and feasted. Ramona said that if Señor Johnston did not return very soon, she would not be able to make the wedding gown in time because Christmas festivities will soon interfere. Lupita said that if Señor Johnston did not return soon, it meant that he must have been suddenly overcome with reason and common sense. We all laughed.

The men talked in hushed tones about war. The women are not allowed to join in the discussions. The thought of war chills my blood.

DECEMBER 13

Señor Johnston returned today, crestfallen and haggard. I led him into the family *sala*, where he sat quietly, twisting his hat in his hands. He has been searching throughout Alta California for white silk material and French ruffles, all in vain. He traveled to Monterey, the capital, then sailed south all the way to San Diego. All he found was a green silk, not a very attractive color. He dreaded giving the news to Miguela. I felt so sorry for him. I decided not to stay in the room and watch him be humiliated. A few minutes later I heard an awful scream and heard running footsteps in the corridor. Miguela flew past, her eyes streaming with tears. The green silk was heaped on the floor. I felt sorry even for headstrong Miguela, for a wedding gown is an important thing.

Señor Johnston said that there was one other place he could search for cloth — Sutter's Fort. Johann Sutter buys supplies from ships the same as Señor Johnston, and though the odds are not good, Sutter may have some white silk in his possession. Johnston left immediately, not even taking one day of rest.

Time is running out. Besides the wedding dress and linens for Miguela, Ramona is making new dresses for Christmas festivities. Poor Ramona is beside herself. I am in charge of sewing Gabriela's new dress. It is a fine blue velvet. I cut up my ruined blue brocade dress, which never washed completely clean of mud stains, and used some of it for the bodice. Gabriela will look beautiful.

DECEMBER 15

La Posada begins tomorrow night. Gabriela has been chosen to play the part of Blessed María this year. She will ride on a burro, and Señor Medina will walk beside her, playing the role of José.

DECEMBER 16

Sewed all morning. After *siesta*, I helped Gabriela dress in a gray wool robe that draped over her head. Señor Medina wore biblical clothing to look like José. Domingo was chosen to be the angel who walks in front of the procession, guiding the way. He wore wings made of wire and chicken feathers, shedding them with every step he took. Angel, indeed! Ha!

We arrived in Sonoma at dusk, in time to join a throng of people who had gathered in the plaza. Bonfires blazed in front of the church, and the houses that would take part in *La Posada* that night. It was very cold.

The procession followed the burro from one designated house to another, portraying José and María looking for lodging in Bethlehem. At each house, decorated with pine branches and blazing with many candles, the procession broke into two groups: one outside the house, the other inside.

The group outside sang this verse as we knocked on the first door:

> *In the name of Heaven*
> *I beg you for lodging,*
> *because She cannot walk,*
> *my beloved wife.*

The group inside the house then answered, singing:

> *This is not an inn,*
> *so keep on going.*
> *I won't open the door,*
> *in case you are a rogue.*

Being turned away, José and María proceeded to the next house, and we sang a different verse begging for lodging, but again those inside turned us away. The procession continued knocking on designated doors until they came to the last house, which was the Vallejo house. As the final verses were sung, the people inside suddenly threw open their doors. The music became more merry. The general himself sang out, surrounded by his wife and children, sisters and brothers-in-law, and friends:

> Enter, holy Pilgrims
> receive this corner;
> for though this dwelling is poor,
> I offer it with all my heart.

We all entered and sang the rest of the verses together around a wonderful Nativity made of carved whale bone. My eyes feasted on the fine furniture — mahogany from the Orient, cherry from Boston, marble from Italy, paintings of ancestors on the long corridor walls, and an old suit of armor worn by a *conquistador* three hundred years ago.

The guests retreated to the *gran sala*, and the finest party I have ever seen commenced. The hot chocolate warmed our insides, and the lively music warmed our hearts. The tables were festooned with colorful garlands of cloth, pine boughs, and flowers. Candelabras hung from the ceilings, and sconces blazed along the hallways, lighting every corner. Golden light bounced off the crystal and silverware and off the jewels of the women as they laughed. The feast before us was fantastic — *buñuelos*, candies, dried fruits, nuts, tamales, meats, breads, wine, *ponche* made from fruit juices, and hot chocolate.

At the Nativity scene with live animals, while the priest was giving a blessing, the ducklings began squawking in the most hilarious manner and one got under his long robe. Not a lip in the house could hide its smile.

Shortly afterward, a group of players performed *pastorelas* — religious plays depicting scenes from the Bible. Finally, the children broke open a star-shaped *piñata* filled with fruits, nuts, and sweet confections. Domingo scrambled on all fours and scooped as much of the booty as he could, using his hat as a basket. I am too old for those childish games, but it is fun to watch Domingo. It was sweet of him to share some of the candy with me.

When the dancing started, Gabriela and I snuggled in a corner and watched the beautiful women and handsome men glide across the floor in graceful waltzes, or shuffle around in lively quadrilles. I cannot wait until I am old enough to dance. Rafaela, who not long ago celebrated her fifteenth birthday, her *quinceañera*, is dancing with men for the first time tonight.

DECEMBER 17

The Medina family will attend *La Posada* in Sonoma every night for the next eight days, until *Nochebuena* — Christmas Eve. But I am too busy to go with them. The servants, *vaqueros*, and laborers have their own *posada* here at the *rancho*. Their clothes may not be as fancy, but the food is good, and the music of Tomás's *guitarra* is unmatched. I love Lupita's round face as she sings in her high-pitched voice. She gets tears in her eyes, and Gregorio holds her hand.

All these Nativity scenes make me think of my own dear mother. I can not help but wonder if she ever participated in *La Posada* or if she celebrated Indian festivals. Sometimes I do not feel that I belong to the Indian world. Nor to the world of the Medinas, either. Where do I belong? Until I find out who my parents were, I know I shall never rest.

DECEMBER 18

The women rode to Sonoma early to help clean and decorate the church for the midnight mass on Christmas Eve. Some Indians are busily building a grand *castillo* in the middle of the plaza for the fireworks on the final night. Domingo was so excited he couldn't sit still and pestered the builders all morning.

DECEMBER 19

¡Gracias a Dios! Señor Johnston returned today, his horse worn to the bone from hurrying back from Sutter's Fort. He found some white silk, but not enough for the full dress. The bodice will have to be made of the plain green. Miguela is upset and pouts about it. I am the one who will sew hundreds of tiny seed pearls over the bodice. By the time I finish, it will look white, indeed.

Gabriela and I overheard Johnston talking to Señor Medina in the library. While at Sutter's Fort, he met an American, Captain John Frémont, and his men.

"Captain Frémont says he is in California merely to survey the land," Johnston explained, "but I'm not so sure."

Señor Medina does not trust Frémont. He thinks the captain is biding his time until the war starts. As soon as Frémont gets word from the United States, he will march on the *californios* with his men and try to seize their lands.

Gabriela and I exchanged worried glances. I know what she was thinking: If we go to war with the *americanos*, which side will the Johnstons take?

DECEMBER 20

Ramona started Miguela's wedding gown. Her eyes are red from the long hours, and she has many interruptions from guests who have come for the Christmas festivities. Every time a button falls off or a hem needs mending or a cuff is torn, poor Ramona is told to put aside the wedding dress and make repairs immediately. I was careless this morning, and before I noticed I had sewn a sleeve of Gabriela's new dress to the neck instead of the sleeve hole. I had to rip the seams and I accidentally tore the cloth. Another sleeve had to be cut, but since there is not enough cloth, it is shorter than the other.

Miguela came in several times today to determine our progress and bellowed her dissatisfaction, threatening to throw Ramona to the wolves if this or that is not corrected. Ramona is beside herself with anguish and frustration. I would not be surprised if she runs away and returns to her people in the hills. If she leaves, I think I will not be far behind her, for the thought of having to complete the wedding dress alone would turn my hair as white as snow.

I am weaving a wool *rebozo* as a Christmas gift for Nelly, though I will not see her until the wedding in January. It is shades of brown, pinks, and yellows, with a streak of blue. I work on it late at night after everyone is asleep until I cannot keep my eyes open. I have decided to sacrifice writing in my diary for a few days until the *rebozo* is completed.

December 23

Lupita and Ramona got into an argument today. Lupita insisted that she needed me to help her in the kitchen to prepare the Christmas feast, while Ramona insisted she needed me to help with the wedding trousseau. The *mayordomo* heard the arguing and called Señora Medina to settle the question. The Señora decided that feeding the guests was more important than the wedding ensembles. When Miguela heard this, she burst into tears and threw a tantrum. Only Miguela could make Christmas an unpleasant occasion.

December 24

At last *Nochebuena* has arrived. The largest *Posada* procession of all — rich and poor alike — walked the street following José and María on the little burro. Just before midnight, our final stop was in front of the massive oak doors of the church. My feet ached in their leather sandals, for it was very cold.

We sang the final verses, then the church doors burst open and everyone rushed inside cheering and singing joyously at midnight. The light of what seemed like a thousand candles lit the church as bright as daylight. The bells pealed until even the sleeping doves flew out the belfry tower.

After Christmas mass, children played games and swung at *piñatas* hung from trees in the plaza. At last the *castillos* were lit, and the sky twinkled with fireworks, whirling and spinning, hissing and exploding. I cannot recall having seen such grand fireworks in all my life. Domingo screamed with joy, but got too close to a firecracker and burned his hand. He took the pain bravely and said it was nothing, but I think it will leave a scar. When I told him so, he was very pleased, saying it is a sign of manhood.

DECEMBER 25

Feliz Navidad. May the world live in peace and forget thoughts of war.

December 26

A large blister rose on Domingo's hand from the burn and pained him terribly for a while. Lupita smeared it with bear grease. He says the scar does not bother him. He wears it like a badge of courage, proudly saying that it will be a reminder of the power of the *castillo*. He said the same thing last year when he was nicked in the shoulder by the horns of a yearling bull, and this autumn past when one of the fighting cocks spurred him along the neck. At this rate of injury, he will be covered with scars like some Indians are covered with tattoos.

January 1, 1846

A new year is upon us. I cannot help but reflect upon the past year and wonder what the new one will bring. Since no one knows what day Domingo or I were born, Padre Ygnacio decreed that we should both celebrate our births on January 1. It is a dreary time of year, but at least it is a date that neither of us ever forgets. As he does every year, Domingo protested that his birth date is shared with mine. I told him he is free to choose any other day he wants. He is going to mull over the problem. This decision, however, did not prevent him from sharing the *pan dulce* that Lupita baked, or from accepting a new pair of leather gloves from Gregorio.

JANUARY 6

Day of Epiphany. Today we celebrate the Feast of the Three Kings, the day the Wise Men brought gifts to baby Jesús in the manger. It is a day of great joy because the children awaken to find sweet treats and small gifts tucked here and there.

I gave Domingo a fine embroidered band for his hat. I gave Gabriela a small embroidered pillow for her bed, made from pieces of the blue brocade and bits left over from Miguela's wedding dress. The design was a green cactus bordered by flowers. Gabriela squealed with delight and hugged me dearly. Then she gave me a ball of perfumed Castilian soap. My heart flew with joy. I know that she has owned the soap for years, but it does not matter.

Gabriela showed me the gifts she received from her parents, aunt and cousins, and godparents. I am pleased that Gabriela chose to share her joy with me, but I cannot help but feel sad that I have no family. Gregorio and Lupita gave me a hair comb carved from abalone shell. Lupita said the girls from her tribe wear this design. It is hard for me to think of Lupita and Gregorio as Indians, for they dress like Spaniards, and they speak perfect Spanish. Lupita lived in missions all her life. Gregorio was born in the hills, a wild-hearted young man. When he was wounded in a battle, he was taken to Mission Solano. Lupita nursed him back to health, and he became a Christian. After the mission closed, they both went to work for Señor Medina. I never hear them speak their native languages.

JANUARY 10

Thank goodness! I finished the beadwork on the bodice of the wedding dress today. It is a miracle that I am not blind from the detailed work. When I close my eyes at night I see tiny seed pearls swirling on a green bodice. All that is lacking on the wedding gown is the hemming of the skirt and sleeves. As for Gabriela's dress, I finished that days ago. Gabriela looks like an angel in the blue cloth. Rafaela's dress is completed also. She tried it on, and it was a bit too large. Ramona swears that Rafaela has lost weight since the first fitting a week ago. Her complexion, always pale, seems even more pale of late. She hardly touched her food at the scrumptious Epiphany dinner.

Now Ramona and I will concentrate on sewing table linens and bed linens. The work is pure tedium! The wedding date is set for January 18, which is a Sunday. There will be a grand feast. Then freedom from Miguela!

SUNDAY, JANUARY 11

Miguela tried on her finished wedding gown today. I will not write what she had to say about the green bodice. Señor Johnston will arrive Thursday. He sent his guest list earlier. It included several Americans, including Captain Frémont whom he met in December. Señor Medina does not trust Frémont, but his Spanish hospitality will not allow him to refuse anyone who comes here.

Local *rancheros* fear that the same thing will happen to California that happened to Texas if *norteamericano* settlers keep moving here. What if a fight breaks out between the *americano* wedding guests and the *californios?* What if someone draws a pistol? I pray not. It would be a pity, for Señor Johnston is a fine man and Miguela is fortunate to have him as a fiancé. I have not seen Walter in weeks. I wonder if he knows how to speak Spanish yet? I cannot wait to see Nelly again and give her the *rebozo* I made.

JANUARY 15

I was awakened at dawn by a loud shriek and the sound of voices in the corridor. Lupita, still in her long nightshirt and her floor-length hair loose around her shoulders, shook me and told me to come to the kitchen. Señorita Rafaela has taken ill. Her mother found her collapsed in the hall and screamed. Gregorio has already left for Sonoma to fetch a doctor.

I helped Lupita cook a hot broth and carried it to Rafaela's room. She lay on her bed, a delicate pale flower against white pillows, almost hidden by the bedcovers. Her long black hair flows around her face loosely like weeds in a river. She breathes heavily, her lungs barely able to take air. Señora Medina sits on the edge of the bed, holding her daughter's hand.

Late in the day, Señor Johnston, Walter, and Nelly arrived with a small wedding party from Yerba Buena. They had passed Gregorio on the road and heard the bad news. The wedding plans are postponed for now.

JANUARY 16

I gave the *rebozo* to Nelly and watched her freckled face ignite with joy. To my grand surprise she gave me a small block of ink as a Christmas gift. I am so glad she is here to share these troubling times.

Rafaela's condition grows worse. The house is in despair. I found Gabriela in the garden weeping. We hugged, and she said she regretted every bad word she had said to Rafaela in her life. I gathered a bouquet of winter roses and put them in Rafaela's room. She has a raging fever and knows nothing of what happens around her.

January 17

Miguela is torn with grief. I suspect it is not just because her sister is deathly ill, but it is also because her wedding plans are being disrupted. Señora Medina's sister, Gertruda, and several neighboring ranchers' wives have arrived to comfort the family. The doctor gave Rafaela what medicine he had, but said that prayers would serve as well as anything.

Señora Medina sent Domingo to Sonoma to get more candles from the priest. Today is the Blessing of the Animals, so Domingo took with him a slew of hound puppies, a cage with three roosters, a *burro*, and a half-lame horse. Though it is usually a fun occasion, I stayed home. Walter went with Domingo, looking sad and uncomfortable. I think all this talk of death reminds him of his parents.

Sunday, January 18

Rafaela's condition worsens daily. The fever has gone into her lungs, which have always been the weakest part of her body. She has had several attacks like this, the first when she was a small child. The doctor says that if she can stay alive a few more days, she has a chance of surviving.

This morning I found Señor Medina in the courtyard sitting on a bench, his head slumped into his hands. Never have I seen him look so broken. My heart leaped into my throat as I stood in front of him, afraid to talk. At last I touched his shoulder. He jumped slightly, then sat up straight. His dark eyes shimmered with tears. "Rosa? Is she gone?"

I shook my head. "No, Señor, but she is calling for you."

"To say good-bye, no doubt." He heaved a long sigh.

I told him that there was still hope. Lupita says her people know of many roots and herbs that cure diseases. These words seemed to suddenly revive his spirit. The white doctors often scoff at the ways of the Indians, but Señor Medina said he was willing to try anything.

Gregorio had already left for Sutter's Fort, hoping to find medicine there, so Lupita set out alone to find her people and bring back the herbs. Señor Medina told me to go with her and gave us his best horses to ride.

January 19

Lupita turned over the kitchen duties to Ramona. Domingo saddled our mounts. He is going with us because he is very good with horses and Lupita is afraid of them. With enough supplies to last a few days, we set off.

We rode all day and met Gregorio riding at a gallop from Sutter's Fort. There was no doctor at the fort, but he had some medicine. He said he would continue back to Rancho Agua Verde with the white man's medicine while Lupita would continue on to her people, another day's ride to the north.

January 20

We rode all day, down hills and over *barrancos*, through the Napa Valley. It was very cold, and a light frost covered the ground. We found Lupita's people at a small *ranchería* that consisted of about a dozen huts made of sticks covered with tree bark and animal skins. The wind blew bitterly, and no one was outside. Smoke rose from the tops of the huts, and the aroma of roasting grain made my mouth water. Lupita went to the hut of the *cacique* — how she knew it was the leader's hut, I do not know. They exchanged greetings, then the *cacique* led us to another hut. It smelled of animal skins, smoke, and dried herbs and roots. The man inside must have been a *shaman*, for he quickly began opening bags of herbs and mixing them together, giving instructions to Lupita all the while. He chanted and shook a stick over the bag of medicine.

We gave the man some calico cloth and some seed pearls left over from Miguela's wedding gown. He seemed pleased at the exchange. As we left the hut, most of the village gathered outside. These few miserable-looking people are all who are left of Lupita's once numerous nation. Most died of diseases. Others slaved at the missions for years until the missions closed down and they had no place to go. They dispersed to work on *ranchos* or returned to the hills to eke out a living in terrible poverty. I think seeing them broke Lupita's heart.

The people wore deer skins lined with pieces of rabbit fur and sat on bearskin rugs. They looked perfectly warm, while I was shivering in my wool dress and *rebozo*. They offered us food, mostly bread made from acorn flour, which I found to be rather bitter, and some kind of fleshy roots. As they talked to Lupita, I could not help but think about my own mother. I wonder if she lived in animal skins and ate acorns. My eyes searched the faces of the crowd, hoping against hope to recognize some of my mother's features among them, but all was futile. As we mounted our horses and headed back to the *rancho*, anxiety overwhelmed my heart. I pray we are not too late.

January 22

We arrived back at the Medina *rancho*, half expecting to see the funeral carriage parked out front. To our great relief, Rafaela was still alive. The white man's medicine had not cured her, but she was hanging by a thread. Lupita quickly prepared the herbs, making a foul-smelling broth and administered it to Rafaela. She coughed and gagged, but finally swallowed it all.

Rafaela coughed up phlegm all day. Tonight she opened her eyes and breathed freely for the first time in a week. Señora Medina wept and hugged her daughter close. Señor Medina had to leave the room to hide his emotion. I saw him go to the family altar, fall on his knees, and clasp his hands in prayer. I saw

Miguela and Gabriela also fall on their knees in thanks, so I did the same. I think every soul on the Medina *rancho* sent their prayers of thanks to the Heavenly Father this night. I am too exhausted from the long ride to write more.

January 24

Señor Johnston had to return to Yerba Buena on urgent business. Nelly and Walter went with him. They will come back for the wedding, whose date no one knows. It saddens me to see Nelly go, but I will see her again soon.

January 26

The *mayordomo*, Señor Villareal, returned today from a lengthy business trip to Monterey, where he was making arrangements for the sale of cattle hides, tallow, and handicrafts. He missed the turmoil caused by Rafaela's illness. The sight of the little man reminded me once again that he had seen me in Señor Medina's library reading a book of poems.

This afternoon, while Lupita was busy with Rafaela, Señor Villareal entered the kitchen holding a ledger. I wanted to run, but the pots were boiling. He asked about the flour supply, the beans, the corn, and so forth. He stared at me a long time, as if trying to remember who I was. When he left, I had the feeling that he had remembered the incident in the library. Now I am afraid to face Señor Medina. I've decided the best thing for me is to avoid him.

JANUARY 28

A strange thing happened today. I got into a squabble with Domingo when he brought a hound pup into the kitchen. Domingo grabbed my arm and tore my sleeve. I was furious, but Domingo managed to duck my wooden spoon. I was stomping down the corridor on the way to the sewing room to make repairs when Señor Medina suddenly appeared at his library door and called to me in a firm voice. My heart was in my throat, and all thoughts of ripped sleeves fell aside. I slipped inside, one hand holding the torn sleeve, the other hand shaking nervously by my side. I stood in front of his massive desk covered with documents, ledgers, bottles of ink, and feather quills.

I expected to hear that the *mayordomo* had finally revealed my crime of reading the book of poetry. For a moment Señor Medina was silent, then unexpectedly he said, "What is wrong with your arm?" Shocked at his words, I glanced up to see his dark eyes focused on my hand.

I told him it was just a silly accident; that Domingo had torn my sleeve while we were scuffling. I dropped my hand and allowed the sleeve to fall aside so he could see the damage. I wanted him to chastise Domingo.

Señor Medina at first smiled, then his eyes squinted. He walked around the desk and asked to see my arm. I was embarrassed, for proper ladies do not expose any part of their limbs to men or boys, but it was an order. I lifted my arm, and he leaned closer. "Where did you get that scar?" he asked.

"Why, I've had it as long as I can remember, and I do not know what caused it. Domingo has one exactly like it in the same place. It may have been an Indian ritual our mother performed on us."

But Señor Medina shook his head. "No, it isn't

that. I see now why you and Domingo survived the smallpox epidemic that killed your mother. That is a smallpox vaccination on your arm. The padre must have administered it."

I could not believe my ears. I assured Señor Medina that Padre Ygnacio did not do such a thing. He always thought it was a miracle we lived. I asked him what the scar meant.

"It means that someone cared about you deeply. Someone with power and influence." With these words, he dismissed me, apparently forgetting why he had called me inside the room.

JANUARY 29

I did not sleep well last night. Señor Medina's words haunted me. If my white father had cared enough to get his children smallpox vaccinations, then why did my mother not also get one? Why is she dead and her children alive? Why didn't my father come for his children at the mission? Padre Ygnacio had called Domingo and me his little *milagros* — miracles. Now I see that it was not a miracle at all that we survived, merely the white man's medicine. I feel as if something precious, a part of me, has been taken away. Before, I felt as if I had been chosen by God, that I had survived the terrible plague by His own hand. Now I no longer feel special. I am not sure I will tell Domingo this news.

JANUARY 30

Señor Medina called me into his office again. I trembled with fear, anticipating that he had discovered some new horrible secret about my past and was going to dismiss me from service. He got to the point immediately.

"Rosalia, the *mayordomo* insists that he saw you in my library reading a book. I told him that was impossible; that surely you were simply gazing at the illustrations. Now, tell me, is that what happened?"

I felt sick inside. I was taught it is a sin to lie, yet he had given me an easy escape. My head roared that I should take the escape, but my heart roared that I should tell the truth. I began to tremble. The señor's eyes softened, and a slight smile touched his lips, encouraging me. I took a deep breath and told him the truth. That I had read his books; that Padre Ygnacio taught me to read at the mission; that I kept a diary.

Señor Medina leaned back in his chair, a look of total amusement on his face. "Unbelievable," he whispered, then he leaned over and selected a book from the nearest shelf, a book about Napoléon and the art of war. He opened it to a random page and bade me read.

I read nervously, stumbling over many words, but in all, it was a good reading. Señor Medina shook his head. "Amazing!" He closed the book.

I still cannot believe Señor Medina's parting words: "I have decided that you and Domingo will receive lessons with Gabriela. Perhaps your presence will inspire her to study. You will begin after Candlemas."

JANUARY 31

I am still in shock. When I told Domingo that we are to receive lessons, he created a dozen excuses why he was too busy to attend. He screamed his protest as he ran out the kitchen to the stables. When I told the news to Gabriela, she was thrilled to have someone to share the boredom of Señor Gordillo and his theories of multiplication.

FEBRUARY 2

Today is *La Candelaria* — Candlemas Day. We rode to Sonoma for the mass and the parade of candles. The priest gave a grand sermon, retelling the story of María and José bringing baby Jesús to the temple forty days after his birth for the purification ceremony. The priest blessed everyone's candles, and we had a good parade. It was a very cold day, and the wind played havoc with everyone's candle. The saying goes that if your candle blows out on Candlemas, you will have bad luck the rest of the year. If so, then all of us are doomed.

After mass we released doves and celebrated. Colorful lanterns hung from every house rafter, swaying in the wind. A few Americans were there, including Jacob Leese, who is married to General Vallejo's sister and lives in town in a fine house. Señor Leese, who speaks Spanish very well, told the children an amusing story.

He said that German settlers in the United States believe that on this day a little furry animal called a groundhog will come out of his den. If the sun is shining, he will be frightened by his shadow, run back inside to sleep six more weeks, and winter will continue. But if it is cloudy, he will not go back to sleep and the remaining winter will be mild. Señor Leese recited an interesting poem:

> *If Candlemas be fair and bright,*
> *Winter still has a lot of fight.*
> *If Candlemas brings clouds and rain,*
> *Winter will not come again.*

Domingo and the other boys laughed hysterically at the story of the groundhog. They decided to go up and down the *barrancos* looking for a similar animal. They came back two hours later with a badger in a sack, but it got the best of them and chewed a hunk out of Domingo's thumb. Now he has yet another scar to remind him of his bravery.

FEBRUARY 3

My lessons began today. Señor Gordillo is as round as a pumpkin and seems far more interested in what Lupita is cooking in the kitchen than what is in the books he brought. Since I already know how to read and write, he told me to read a book to Gabriela and Domingo. While I did so, Señor Gordillo took a nap behind the couch. Señor Medina is wasting his money!

FEBRUARY 4

Señor Johnston arrived to discuss the wedding date. Miguela greeted him coolly. For his sake, I pray she does not wait until the wedding day to change her mind.

Señor Johnston wants the wedding to take place immediately and cares little for ceremonies. But every date he selected was rejected because of religious fiestas. They argued some more, and when Johnston finally left, the wedding date had been set for February 14, the last Saturday before Lent. Miguela is pouting. She wanted a spring wedding, with wildflowers and pleasant weather. In February, it is bound to be raining.

Lupita shook her head. "If they cannot agree on a wedding date, how will they ever agree on things of importance?" What a marriage that will be!

FEBRUARY 5

All morning I strung red chiles into long *ristras* and hung them from beams to dry. Señora Medina's sister, Gertruda, was visiting with her children. While my back was turned, the youngest little boy got a fistful of chiles and stuck them into his mouth. His screams brought the household running. Naturally I was blamed. For punishment Lupita has put me in charge of slopping the pigs for one week. I must carry reeking buckets of sour milk and food scraps to the foul-smelling pigsty. The pigs squeal and grunt as they fight over the slop. Their sides fill up like bellows as they gorge themselves. I found a runt piglet half buried in the mud. The mother sow has rejected it, and it is barely alive. I gave it to Domingo. He feeds it goat's milk through the finger of a glove with a small hole. Its name is Pequito, for it is very small.

February 6

I am at my wit's end. I thought lessons would be wonderful, but I am in tears at the end of each day. True, I know how to read and write, but I am as ignorant as a *burro* when it comes to ciphering numbers. And history makes my head ache. I marvel that Señor Gordillo's breeches do not split open every time he stoops. He breaks for food six times a day and always smells like *tamales* and *tortillas*. He uses food for all the arithmetic demonstrations — *uno, dos, tres, cuatro, cinco* grapes drop into the bowl; then, to demonstrate subtraction, *uno, dos, tres, cuatro, cinco* grapes vanish into his mouth. It is the only part of lessons that Domingo likes. He has learned his subtraction very well, I must admit.

February 9

Three men rode to the *rancho* all the way from Monterey through rainy weather. I had to leave my lessons and clean their long *ponchos* and footgear.

While I sat on the veranda scrubbing mud from the leather boots and heavy spurs, I listened to their worried voices drifting through the opened windows. They brought news of great concern. In late December, the United States annexed Texas and made it into a state, just as everyone feared.

"Surely this will mean war with the United States," Señor Gordillo said in his husky voice. "Mexico will never ignore such an insult to her honor."

The arguing raged. If war does come, where will California stand? Do *californios* owe their allegiance to Mexico, who has treated them like an unwanted orphan? Should they fight the *americanos* who are now on their soil?

Some agreed with Señor Medina that the Mexican government does not care about California. It does not send soldiers to protect us from Indian atrocities. It does not send money to establish ports and settle towns. Everything *californios* have was earned by their own efforts. Even the soldiers are trained and paid out of the pockets of General Vallejo.

A shout rose up: "Why should *californios* fight a war for a mother country that considers us a distant, barren land? We should follow the example of Texas and declare our independence. Let us become a republic."

The men moved into the parlor and closed the door, so I heard no more of their conversation. But my fingers still shake at the thought of a war here on the soil of California.

FEBRUARY 11

It has been a madhouse all week. Lessons have been suspended so every free hand can help to prepare for the wedding. No more time to write.

FEBRUARY 12

Spent the day sweeping and scrubbing tiles, dusting rugs and curtains, and ironing linens for the guest beds. Thank goodness we are having a warm spell. I pray that it will not rain on Saturday. Indian workers have been cutting timber to build a huge brush *ramada* under which the main festivities will occur. Domingo is helping pour wine from wooden vats into smaller vessels. Miguela paces the floor like an angry puma. Señora Medina should put a chain on her door to keep Miguela from bolting before Saturday.

February 13

The last of the guests arrived this morning, including Señor Johnston, Nelly, and Walter. Nelly and I hugged and squealed. She helped me grind dried corn on the *metate*, pat out *tortillas*, and make *tamales*.

All evening, Señor Johnston paced the floor like Miguela, tugging at his droopy mustache and smoking one cigar after another. He said Americans believe that Friday the thirteenth means bad luck. I wanted to tell him that his luck would be grand if Miguela canceled. I hear distant thunder. The air smells of rain.

It is late now. Rafaela just walked past the kitchen door in her long white nightgown, looking more like a ghost than a girl. Her black hair hangs past her waist in thick tangles. She is coming; I must stop writing for now.

Later

Rafaela just left. She requested a bowl of soup and a piece of bread. I am so pleased to see her eating and walking again. But her large eyes are mournful, like those of a wounded doe. I asked her why she was so sad, and she said:

"I am happy for Miguela, but I cannot help but think that no man will ever marry me. I am too weak and sickly. I do not blame Señor Johnston for choosing Miguela and her strong body, but still, my heart aches." Then she leaned her head down on the table and wept right among the squash and beans.

I didn't know what to do, so I told her she was a beautiful, kind girl and that if she would eat more and have a better constitution and gain some strength, she would have her pick of suitors. She needs to go outside more — walk in the garden, ride a horse. Miguela rides like a man. Maybe that is what makes her so strong.

Rafaela sniffed, then hugged me. "Rosa, thank you," she said, and vowed to go outdoors more. I hope I did not give her false hope.

FEBRUARY 14

¡Gracias a Dios! The wedding is over. Señorita Miguela is now Señora Johnston. The wedding party

rode to Sonoma under low, threatening black clouds early in the morning. Miguela, who was as beautiful as an angel, went through the ceremony without a squawk. A sigh of relief passed over the Medina family, the guests, and especially Señor Johnston.

It began storming just as the party arrived back at the *rancho*. Wind and hail foiled their fun, and all the outdoor festivities have been canceled for now. Domingo is so disappointed that the fireworks fizzled and misfired. The food was moved indoors from under the *ramada*, and a grand celebration with music, food, drinking, and dancing commenced in the *gran sala*. I wish I could stay awake all night, but there is much work to be done tomorrow, so I must retire.

Sunday, February 15

Still raining. The horse races that were scheduled for today were canceled, although a few brave *caballeros* rode in the pouring rain. The game in which a rooster is buried in the sand and the rider tries to scoop its head off in one bold jerk was canceled, too. I am glad. I always feel sorry for the roosters. A cockfight was held under the *ramada* until the roof caved in and drenched the men. They had a good laugh.

The guests were supposed to be outside all day yesterday and today eating under the *ramada*, with bullocks being barbecued over spits. Instead, the guests are crammed into every corner, demanding food faster than Lupita, Ramona, and I can cook.

At least the dance was a success. The ladies wore the most spectacular dresses, and the men wore suits with silver tiepins and colorful sashes. Gabriela is not allowed to dance with men yet, but I saw several men admiring her. I am proud the dress I sewed turned out beautifully. It is past midnight, and still the guitars and violins sing. Too tired to write more.

February 16

Lupita and I rose at four in the morning to begin preparing food. The rain did not let up all day, so those guests who had planned to leave did not. Coffee supply is low. I have been too busy to visit with Nelly. Señora Medina insisted that Nelly stay out of the kitchen and talk to some young men. I know Nelly did not want to do it, but she had little choice.

FEBRUARY 17

The rain stopped, and the wedding festivities ended. The bride and groom left, their horses' hooves kicking up mud onto their clothes. Everyone formed a procession and followed them as far as Sonoma, where they will spend the night before going on to Yerba Buena. Everyone cheered and threw flowers as the couple rode by. Boys threw *cascarónes*, eggshells filled with perfumed water.

Rafaela has just knocked at my door and said her father wishes to speak to me in the morning. I am too tired to worry about what he wants this time.

FEBRUARY 18

I am still in shock at what Señor Medina said to me today. He looked almost as tired as me, and I knew he was very glad that the festivities were over and he could continue with the business of running his *rancho*. Expecting him to make some comment about my lessons, or my smallpox vaccination, I was not prepared for his words:

"Rafaela has requested that you become her personal servant."

As Rafaela's personal servant my duties would be to wait on her and accompany her wherever she wishes. I would no longer have to work in the kitchen or sew clothes. My sole duty would be as companion to Rafaela. The physician had told Señor Medina that Rafaela needs to spend more time outdoors, walking in the garden, riding about the hills. She cannot do such things alone, and her current personal servant, Maricela, is very old and unable to ride.

I was speechless, and barely managed to sputter a few words of thanks. Most servants would cherish such a favored position, but any joy I felt at the promotion was quickly smashed when Señor Medina said that I will no longer be taking lessons.

"I will allow one hour a day for Señor Gordillo to tutor you," he said. "I know this is a disappointment to you, Rosa, but in reality you already have completed more studies than most girls in California. Consider yourself fortunate. I will allocate two of my finest mares for you and Rafaela."

No more lessons! I held back my tears until I reached the kitchen. As I sobbed, my tears fell into the soup. I did not care. I served it to Señor Medina. I hope he tasted the salt.

FEBRUARY 19

Today I began my duties as personal servant to Rafaela. She wants to learn to ride a horse and build her strength so she can go to the top of the nearest hill and look over the valley.

Gabriela is very moody today. During the one hour of lessons that I received this morning, she took her slate board and slate pencil to another spot, putting Domingo between us. She did not look my direction the whole hour and did not speak when I left. But, finally, she confronted me in the hall:

"You were to be my personal servant!" she wailed. "We talked about it often. How could you do this to me?"

"I had no choice. Señor Medina requested it. How could I have said no?"

"*¡Silencio!*" she hissed. "I don't know why I wanted you as a friend, anyway. You're just a servant." She stomped off. Maybe I should not continue my studies since it causes Gabriela so much anguish, but I cannot give them up.

SUNDAY, FEBRUARY 22

I helped Rafaela dress for mass, a dark green and black ensemble with a lacy black *mantilla* that made her skin appear even paler. I rode beside her in the carriage. It was crowded, stuffy, and dusty. I think I prefer riding on a mule, like Domingo. Gabriela sat across from us, her eyes averted toward the window.

This Wednesday begins Lent, and the padre admonished us all to pay penance and lead worthy lives. Each of us is to give up something important during the forty days before Easter as a sign of our faith.

The weather has cleared. Señora Medina declared that tomorrow will be wash day. A week's worth of guests and rain has left every garment, bed linen, tablecloth, and napkin dirty. The servants spent the day removing linens from beds and gathering soiled clothing. Since the Medina women are inclined to wear white with everything, there are many, many pieces to be cleaned. All the servants and the Medina women will participate in the washing. It is more like a *fiesta* than a chore. I cannot wait to bathe in the hot springs.

February 23

We rose long before dawn to prepare food and drink and pack it in baskets. Two Indian servants soaped the wheels of the *carreta* to make them turn easier, then they tied bundles of linens and clothes onto the backs of horses and mules. Señora Medina and her daughters rode at the head of the line in the cart, then came the string of packhorses, each led by an Indian, and behind them walked the women and girls who do the washing. We are fortunate to have hot springs two miles from the ranch that serve well for scrubbing clothes and are enjoyable for swimming, too.

Our caravan moved slowly. There are no roads,

only ruts worn by the wagons. Servants walked alongside the oxen prodding them with a pole. We passed by the main wheat field, which is closed in on three sides by a fence made of the bleached skulls and long horns of slaughtered cattle. The fourth side is fenced by a hedge of tall, prickly pear cactus, called *nopal*. These cactus clumps cannot be penetrated by deer, cattle, or any other living thing. The cactus also produces bright red tuna fruits. These are delicious to eat, but they are covered with hairlike needles that can get into your fingers and cause great pain, as Domingo quickly found out. In the dim morning light the skulls took on an eerie look, and the cries of coyotes added to the frightfulness.

The sun was up when we arrived at the hot springs. I could hear the gurgling and see steam rising from the rocks even before we crested a steep incline and looked down. The distant hills looked blue in the morning mist, and herds of cattle and horses lazily grazed on the slopes. Surely this is the most beautiful place on earth!

The tedious job of washing began. The women unloaded the horses at the upper part of the springs, where the water is clearer. They put Domingo in charge of taking the horses to a pasture to graze on wild oats. We dipped the clothes and linens into the warm water, slathered them with lye soap until suds rose, then rubbed them against smooth rocks until they were clean. Clean pieces were spread on low shrubs or rocks to dry in the warm sun. Afterward, the women washed their long hair in the springs, using yucca roots for soap.

A wash-day group from another *rancho* arrived not long after we did. An old señora, pale and sickly, had come along to bathe in the springs for her health. At the lower end of the springs the water turns to warm mud. They scooped a hole for the old woman and "buried" her up to her neck, where she stayed the entire day, with a little roof of leaves over her head for protection.

The children ran and splashed each other. Everyone was in a gay mood. We had a lovely picnic and slept soundly for *siesta* while the clothes dried. I awoke to the sound of Domingo shouting and pointing to a line of Indians on the hilltop. My heart leaped into my throat. Hostile Indians still occasionally attack *rancheros*, but the leader of the group, a tall, distinguished man, waved, and we realized that it was Chief Solano, leader of the Suisun people. Once fierce and famous for his ability to defeat anyone, when he met General Vallejo as a young soldier, they fought but eventually struck a close friendship and have been allies ever since. The chief took the name Solano from the mission at Sonoma. He is a common sight at the Vallejo mansion and watches over the general's interest. We waved and he left.

When the dried linens had been folded and placed back on the packhorses, we returned home. It was growing dark and cool. The small children fell asleep in their mothers' arms. Gabriela and Rafaela fell asleep in the cart. We sang hymns that echoed over the hills. I know everyone will sleep well tonight.

February 24

Tomorrow Lent begins. Lupita prepared the most marvelous of meals, with fine meat and spicy dressing. The feast was prepared outside and served to all the laborers on the *rancho*.

Keeping company with the same person all day is taxing my nerves. Today Señor Medina presented Rafaela and me with well-trained mares. Rafaela's is a beautiful white Andalusian. Mine is a dappled gray. Gregorio showed us how to saddle and bridle the horses, though it is a chore that I doubt Rafaela will ever have to perform herself. Domingo is very excited at the prospects of going with us on riding excursions. I made Rafaela walk around the garden three times today. She is getting stronger every day, but still far below what a normal girl should be.

ASH WEDNESDAY, FEBRUARY 25

Lent began today. Señora Medina rose up before dawn, dressed herself all in black, and began praying at the altar in the family *sala*. She had already been there for two hours when the rest of the family joined her.

At breakfast each person in the room announced what sacrifice he would make during Lent. Gabriela said she would not play with her dolls. Domingo said he would give up school lessons. Señor Medina frowned, but accepted. Lupita gave up *pan dulce*; Señor Medina sacrificed cigars. When it came my turn, I knew what sacrifice I had to make: my diary. I will write only one entry per week during Lent, on each Sunday. Señor Medina nodded and touched my shoulder. "*¡Bueno!*" he whispered.

We rode to Sonoma to attend mass. The chapel was draped in black, and everyone wore old, ragged clothes. The padre smeared ashes onto the foreheads of the people who attended. Some lashed their own backs with whips until blood stained their clothes.

SUNDAY, MARCH 1

My first entry since Ash Wednesday. The weather has been fine. Rafaela and I walked around the courtyard three times every day, and her lungs are stronger. She walks to the stables to stroke the horses, but only rides a few moments at a time. She is terrified of horses! How cruel is Fate, to be the daughter of a *ranchero* who raises some of the finest horses in California, and to be given a beautiful mare that any human would covet. I look forward to riding the hills. I must be patient. I feel it is only a matter of time until Rafaela will come to love riding. My horse loves to nip at my dress sleeves and hair ribbons.

On Friday, visitors said that American forces under the command of General Zachary Taylor are massed along the Rio Grande in Texas, poised for war with Mexico. Domingo is full of fire and claims he would love to shoot an American. Gregorio twisted his ear and told him war was the worst thing that could happen to a boy.

SUNDAY, MARCH 8

The first week of Lent has passed. Gabriela is speaking to me again. She said that Lent is not the proper time for a person to hold a grudge. She has forgiven Rafaela for asking me to be her personal servant; she has forgiven her father for allowing it; and she has forgiven me for accepting the offer, though in truth, I never wanted the position.

I miss being in the kitchen with Lupita chattering away. Rafaela loves to embroider. She could easily spend her entire day in front of the fire pulling needle and thread in silence. It is only because I insist on our daily walks that she puts the cloth aside. I miss my lessons terribly, but at least I am pleased that Rafaela is growing stronger. She is now able to walk two miles to the nearest hill, view the valley below, and walk back. Her pale cheeks are getting rosy. She is not a bad companion, though not as lively as Gabriela.

SUNDAY, MARCH 15

The second week of Lent passed uneventfully, but after mass today in Sonoma there was great excitement around the Vallejo family. A strange man was standing next to the general, bowing and speaking with a heavy German accent. He is a piano teacher by the name of Andrew Hoeppneu and has been hired to teach the Vallejo children, the general, and his wife how to play. The Vallejos invited everyone to their house for a demonstration.

I've been told that in all of Alta California there are only three pianos and the Vallejos own one of them. Everyone crowded into his *gran sala* to hear the German play. The servants stayed out in the corridor, but we heard the music perfectly. It was a marvel. Never have I heard anything so beautiful and stirring. Gabriela and Rafaela are bursting with envy because they, too, want to learn to play the piano.

SUNDAY, MARCH 22

The third week of Lent was rainy, foggy, and miserable until today, which opened clear and glorious.

Gabriela, Rafaela, Domingo, and I packed a picnic basket and rode a few miles to a tall hill. From its peak you can clearly see most of the Sonoma Valley. The wild mustard is aglow with yellow flowers; golden poppies are coming up everywhere.

Domingo's runt pig, Pequito, is growing nicely. Lupita kiddingly said we will have pork loins for Easter. Domingo ran outside. I found him in the pigpen, Pequito scooped in his arms, and his eyes wet with tears. He loves that pig, and that pig loves him. I assured him that Lupita was just joking, and promised that no harm would come to his precious Pequito.

Sunday, March 29

The fourth week of Lent has passed. Everyone is becoming thin from a meatless diet. Sometimes my mouth waters for the taste of beef. I have dropped at least five pounds; so has everyone in the house, except for Rafaela. She is gaining weight, for her appetite is stronger than it has been in years. She devours three bowls of soup, where once she could barely eat one. Lupita says it is the walking and the fresh air.

Señor Medina will leave for Monterey tomorrow. There is to be an important meeting of all the leaders of Alta California. They will discuss what course to take for the future of California. Some leaders want California to be an independent republic, like Texas once was. Others feel that California is too weak and disorganized to survive on its own like that — we do not even have an army, or funds to raise one. These men want California to give herself to a foreign power and become a province of England or France or the United States. General Vallejo leans toward the Americans, saying they will take California if they want it, anyway. I cannot imagine being an American. All this talk of war makes my flesh crawl.

PALM SUNDAY, APRIL 5

Last week was Passion Week. We spent most of our free time preparing the family altar. Rafaela made beautiful paper decorations while I gathered chamomile flowers, lilies, and roses. On Friday, Lupita and Ramona brought out a replica of Our Lady of Sorrows made out of bread and placed it on the top rung of the altar. I dipped fresh candles, and Domingo carved tiny wooden figures and animals to represent the story of Salvation. The altar was very nice. Several guests who arrived today commented on it.

Today marks the beginning of *Semana Santa* — Holy Week. This morning Indians and *californios* alike walked in a long procession down the streets of Sonoma carrying palm leaves and large wooden crosses. A man dressed like Jesús rode on a *burro* in front of the procession that moved toward the old mission chapel. During mass, the padre blessed the palm leaves which will later be burned and the ashes scooped up and used for next year's Ash Wednesday.

HOLY SATURDAY, APRIL 11

The last day of Lent. Señora Medina, Rafaela, Gabriela, and I have spent this past Holy Week at her sister's house in Sonoma so that my mistress can be closer to the church and all the activities during this most holy of weeks.

On Wednesday evening, we attended the Vespers

of Darkness, in which the padre told the story of the disciples forsaking Jesús. Señora Medina and her sister wept bitterly as altar boys lit candles and then extinguished one after each Psalm was sung.

On Holy Thursday there was a reenactment of the Last Supper and through all the mass, the traditional greeting of "peace" was omitted as a reminder of the betrayal of Judas. That night began the silence of the church bells. They will not sound again for three days.

Yesterday, on Good Friday, a re-creation of the Way of the Cross was given, with almost everyone in the town playing a role. A strong man, who grew a beard for the occasion, dressed in a white robe and carried the heavy wooden cross on his back in a procession, stumbling three times. Afterward, he was bound to the timbers, and a crown of thorns pressed to his head. He cried in such agony that small children begin to cry, not knowing what was happening. I think I saw blood coming down his temples, and felt chills. Not an eye in the audience did not weep.

Today is Holy Saturday, the time for the solemn vigil at the tomb of Christ. A dark, cheerless mass was held this night, with a candle lit by each person. Afterward, we gathered in the plaza and watched a row of hanging *piñatas* made to look like Judas. Inside each had been placed gunpowder, and soon the images were blown to pieces in rapid succession, much to the delight of Domingo. Tomorrow is Easter Sunday. From that day forth I will write in my diary as much as I please.

Señor Medina has returned from Monterey and the political assembly. He says there is nothing but arguing and discontent among the representatives. He fears that California is doomed to be the puppet of a foreign power. The question is: which one?

EASTER SUNDAY, APRIL 12

Pascua de Resurrección, Glorious Sunday. The mission chapel was packed with *rancheros*, servants, and Indians. Even Gregorio and Señor Medina, who avoid churches, attended and took Holy Communion. The church bells sounded in riotous joy after a three-day silence, their loud peals echoing over the valley and scaring the horses and mules.

After mass, the Medina family returned home to

enjoy Lupita's finest meal. I have never tasted meat so grand. We all ate far too much. I am exhausted. Gregorio says that soon it will be time for the *herraderos* — the roundup and branding of the young bulls. Every year, Señor Medina offers a prize to the *vaquero* who displays the best talents in certain riding or roping skills. Domingo is determined to win a prize for riding a bull. I told him he is as stubborn as a bull. Señor Medina has sent for a bullfighter from Monterey. This news has caused a great deal of excitement.

April 14

Rafaela now actually enjoys riding her horse every day. Today Señor Medina joined us, and we rode the farthest we've ever gone. Near a small creek on the far side of his lands we came upon a family of American settlers building a house out of logs and mud.

Everyone in the family was thin. The three children looked so hungry as they hid behind their mother's skirt that Rafaela and I gave them most of our food. The mother thanked us very earnestly. The bearded man with his sleeves rolled up was working very hard plowing the earth with a scraggly mule.

Though Señor Medina explained that it was his land, after some negotiating he agreed to sell the man forty acres and allow him to pay it back after his first crop came in. They shook hands. I can still see the dirty faces.

APRIL 15

The weather is glorious. The snows in the Sierras are melting, and the creeks run with icy waters, the finest I have ever tasted. Domingo swam in the cold waters to impress Rafaela, and now he has a stuffy nose and fever. If he misses *el rodeo* — the rounding up of the cattle — he will never forgive himself.

APRIL 18

All the *vaqueros* left to round up the young cattle from nearby pastures and hills for branding. They will be gone for many days. Lupita is nervous, for many a *vaquero* has been hurt at roundup time. Gregorio has scars to prove the danger. Domingo wanted to go, but his fever is too high. Gregorio told him to stay. Domingo is filled with remorse for being so foolish. I cannot help but pity him. I made him his favorite spicy soup, but even that did not raise his spirits.

Sunday, April 19

Domingo was not in his bed this morning. Lupita is furious and hysterical at the same time. Señor Medina rode off after breakfast to look for him. There is no doubt in anyone's mind that Domingo has gone to find the *vaqueros*. I am sick with worry, for the hills are alive with panthers and bears. Domingo is a great bother sometimes, but he is my only flesh and blood.

April 20

Señor Medina rode up with Domingo comfortably nestled in the saddle in front of him. They were singing and laughing just like a father and son on a pleasant ride. Domingo had not gotten very far because his horse threw him and ran away. Lupita smothered my brother with kisses, and so did I. His fever is gone now, and he eats like a starving pig. Señor Medina did not punish Domingo; instead, he promised to take Domingo to a cockfight at the *rancho* of Señor Duran, whose roosters are renowned throughout Alta California. This has made Domingo forget about *el rodeo*, at least for the moment.

APRIL 22

Domingo and Señor Medina have been pampering his prize rooster, Paladin, and preparing him for the fight, which is to be this Saturday. Paladin resides in a large, luxurious cage, where he struts about and is fed by hand like a king. Paladin's feathers are shades of orange and copper arranged in a most attractive pattern over his huge, muscular body, with beautiful iridescent blue-black tail plumes. His red comb and the red wattle under his chin are trimmed down, giving him an eerie, sleek look. Paladin has been an undefeated champion for three years and earned much money and honor. But he is getting old, and everyone knows it is but a matter of time when he will be killed, or worse still, turn his back and refuse to fight.

Señor Medina asked me to polish the razor-sharp silver blades that will be attached to Paladin's spurs during the fight. They are kept in a small ivory box, wrapped in velvet like precious jewels.

April 25

The men have gone to the *rancho* of Señor Duran for the cockfights. The Medina women stayed home. A lady does not attend such things. Domingo was bursting with pride to be the señor's companion. They secured Paladin in a cage mounted on the back of a mule, as if he were a passenger of high prestige.

Sunday, April 26

The men returned home. Undefeated Paladin received a serious wound, so he will fight no more. He will retire and live out his life with the hens. Señor Medina gave Domingo a young fighting cock to raise for himself. Domingo named him Señor Valeroso, for he will be strong and brave.

Señora Medina received a message from Señor

Johnston saying that he and Miguela will be happy to attend the annual branding of the bulls. The señora is brimming with happiness. So am I at the thought of seeing Nelly again. I wonder if Walter speaks Spanish by now.

May 1

Preparations for the *herraderos* have begun. At the *plaza de toros*, Indian workers are constructing a wooden platform for the musicians and bleachers for spectators. They are also repairing fencing, to make sure that no bull will be able to crash through the walls and escape its fate.

Señora Medina is busy overseeing the sweeping, cleaning, and preparing of the guest rooms. I asked Rafaela if I could help with the work. She said she did not understand why, but begrudgingly gave permission. Lupita has sent to Sonoma for flour and sugar to make special cakes. The weather is warm. I hope it is not as hot as it was last year.

❧❧ ❧

Sunday, May 3

I discovered that Domingo allows his pig, Pequito, to sleep with him. He made me promise not to tell Lupita. I think the smell will let her know soon.

May 8

Señor Johnston, Miguela, and Nelly arrived this evening just before dinner, covered with dust and exhausted from the long ride. The sisters embraced and kissed and seemed truly glad to see each other. Miguela has changed; she even hugged me tightly and said, "Oh, Rosalia, I miss you and Domingo so much." It was the most joyous reunion I have seen in my life.

Nelly and I hugged like sisters. Walter is even more handsome than I remembered. He has the start of a tiny soft mustache that makes him look older than his sixteen years. He smiled and kissed my hand just like a gentleman would do, and said, "*Buenas tardes, Señorita.*" It pleases me beyond words to know that he has learned enough of my language to carry on a bit of conversation. I wish I had worn my blue skirt instead of the ugly brown one. And I discovered later that I had flour in my hair!

I showed Nelly to her room, a small but comfortable nook able to accommodate a bed, washstand, mirror, and small armoire. It has no fireplace, but since the weather is deliciously mild, there is no need. Nelly insisted that I share the room with her and convinced Lupita that it was all right.

At dinner, Johnston lifted a goblet of wine and proudly announced that Miguela is with child. Señora Medina gasped with delight. She put her hands over her mouth, and tears filled her eyes. Señor Medina toasted both of them.

May 9

Nelly said she does all the housework for Señor Johnston and Miguela. She feels beholden to her uncle Henry and will do anything he asks. I know she does not care for Miguela, but she did not say so.

The *herraderos* festivities began with a dinner for the guests, who have been arriving all day in carriages, carts, wagons, on horseback or by mule. Many

Indians have come, too, and are camped under the open sky near the *plaza de toros*. The smell of their stew pots and roasting meat drifts to the balconies and verandas of the *casa grande*. They have set up blankets under trees with handcrafted goods, hoping to make a good swap.

Nelly brought me another block of ink. How sweet of her to remember my diary. She said she started one but lost interest in it within a week. I am too exhausted to write another word.

SUNDAY, MAY 10

The *vaqueros* are back. When we heard Gregorio's voice this morning, Domingo ran into the kitchen and threw his arms around the man's neck. He smells like cattle and dust. His chin is prickly and his hands calloused. He kissed Domingo's face and nodded at me. It is obvious he loves Domingo like a son. I would be happy if he were my father, but he is not.

MAY 11

The guests set out early in the morning and arrived at the *plaza de toros*, where the *vaqueros* were already assembled. People come from leagues around, for Señor Medina's *herraderos* hold a grand reputation in the region.

The hired musicians were seated on a platform playing lively music while guests climbed onto the raised seating areas, the ladies on one side, the gentlemen on another. The ladies' gowns and headpieces twinkled in the morning sun as the ladies fanned themselves with elaborate fans. The gentlemen wore finely crafted leather pants, embroidered jackets with silver buttons, enormous hats to shade out the sun and, as always, the colorful *sarapes* slung over their shoulders. The poorer women wore white blouses, dark skirts, and colorful *rebozos*.

Outside the plaza, every tree was filled with Indians and boys seeking a good spot. I sat between Rafaela and Nelly with a perfect view. The crowd stood and cheered when the herd of bulls was driven in from the nearest field by the *vaqueros*, shouting and whistling, and brandishing their *lazos*. The beasts bellowed so loud that, combined with the thunder of their hooves, you could hardly hear your nearest friend speaking. The bulls were driven into a large corral. From there the *vaqueros* separated them out using well-trained horses and drove them into the main plaza. If the bull snorted and showed good character and stubbornness, the crowd cheered, but if the bull cowered and tried to run, the crowd hissed.

The skill of the *vaqueros* is amazing. Their *lazos* twirl in the air in a great circle over their heads, then fly toward the heels of yearlings. The rope is pulled tight, knocking the helpless animal to the ground. There it is held securely while the hot iron is pressed against its hump, branding it for the Medina *rancho*.

In addition to the branding, the *vaqueros* display their skills. Some ride unbroken *mesteños*, horses captured from wild herds. Other men tackle bulls from horseback by reaching down and grabbing the bull's tail and knocking it off balance while riding at full gallop across the plaza. This feat always causes great cheers. The horses are as talented as the *vaqueros*, standing still when needed, or pushing a bull, all without any noticeable command from the rider.

The music, the laughter, the shouts of the *vaqueros* — it is wonderful! At dusk, everyone returned to the house. A *fandango* is about to begin. I am allowed to attend as a companion to Nelly. Gabriela has generously loaned me a dress. It has shades of red, gold, and black. I am nervous, indeed, for I am not skilled in the social graces and would die if a young man spoke to me, especially a young man like Walter Johnston!

LATER

It is past one o'clock in the morning, and the guitars still sing. The Medinas and their guests will stay up as late as they want, but I must rise with the sun. My heart still pounds at the memory of tonight's festivities. *I did not want to leave.* Nelly, Gabriela, and I sat in a corner, sipping on delicious fruit punch and nibbling *pan dulce*. We admired the fabulous gowns of the women and the fine suits of the gentlemen as they gracefully swept across the floor.

Señor Johnston cut a fine figure, but did not know all the Spanish dances. He came over to us, sipping on his glass of wine, his face flushed from all the activity. He asked Nelly to have a dance with him, but she replied, "I don't know these Spanish dances, Uncle Henry."

Johnston said he would take care of that, then spoke to one of the American guests — there were several at the party. The man borrowed a violin and began to scratch out a fast and lively tune. The Americans cheered, and so did Nelly. "It's a Virginia reel," she said, jumping up. Johnston took her hand, and they joined the Americans who formed two lines, men opposite women. The boisterous dance looked like great fun.

Suddenly I heard a throat being cleared and I looked up into the blue eyes of Walter Johnston. "May I have this dance, Señorita Rosa?" he asked politely.

"I am too young to dance with a boy," I said in a shaky voice.

He frowned. "Well, maybe you're too young to dance to Spanish music, but in America you'd be allowed to dance to a Virginia reel." He held out his hand again. I glanced at Señor Medina, who smiled and nodded.

How my heart pounded and my knees shook as we joined the group. I can still feel the warmth of Walter's hand and the firm grip that led me through the steps. I guess I danced well enough — I did not fall on my face — but I honestly do not recall anything except the smile on Walter's lips and the sweet look in his blue eyes. I shall dream of them all night.

After he danced with me, at the urging of Señor Johnston, Walter asked Rafaela to dance. I do not think he wanted to, but he was polite. Her cheeks blushed red. I am proud that she danced the whole dance without losing her breath. It was the first time I have seen Rafaela enjoy herself at a dance. Señor Medina glanced my direction and winked, as if a secret had passed between us.

May 12

Horse races all day, including one for the women. Some of the *ranchero* wives and daughters are excellent riders. They rode over the same terrain as the men. Shouting in shrill voices and whipping their mounts, they roared down the final stretch. Just as I expected, Miguela was at the lead. Her gray stallion swooped past the finish line a full six lengths ahead of the others. The prize was a pair of fine silver spurs. Señora Medina was aghast that Miguela had raced in her delicate condition and scolded her daughter.

Tomorrow there will be a bullfight and at night fireworks and a final dance. Nelly says she does not want to see a bull killed in front of her eyes. I assured her that once she sees the bravery of the *matador*, she will change her mind.

I cannot sleep. I saw Rafaela and Walter Johnston in the courtyard tonight talking and dancing to a waltz. My heart is sick.

MAY 13

The highlight of this year's spring roundup is *la corrida* — the bullfight. The bulls are strong and some weigh a ton. They have been bred for centuries to be aggressive, brave-hearted, and willing to kill the men who taunt them. We usually do not have a bullfight at the spring roundup, but when Señor Medina learned that the famous Mexican *matador*, Bernardo, was in Monterey visiting his sister, he could not pass up the opportunity. Señor Medina talked Bernardo into coming here, much to the thrill of everyone, for rarely do we see such a professional. He is a seasoned veteran, with a great reputation for his skill and bravery. He arrived at the *casa grande* late at night, so no one saw him. He is very serious and did not partake in the *fandango*.

Early this morning I saw Bernardo on his knees, praying. I was appalled to see Domingo slip in beside him and tug at his sleeve. I did not know whether to call out or leave him alone. When Bernardo stood, I grabbed Domingo.

Bernardo is slender but with muscles as hard as stone. Scars made by the bull's horns run down both hands and on his neck. He smiled and touched Domingo's shoulder. "He is no bother. I did the same when I was his age. He has some wise questions." With that he bowed and left the room.

Domingo had asked the *matador* if he gets afraid before the fight. Bernardo had replied that he is afraid before every fight. Not afraid of dying. Not afraid of being mutilated and crippled for life. Rather, his greatest fear is that he will fail in front of everyone.

LATER

It was a fine afternoon as we rode through trees and wildflowers to the *plaza de toros*, where spectators already filled the stands, trees, and fences. Señor Medina takes great pride in his small herd of fighting bulls. They are more fierce than the bulls seen in the cities of Mexico. Their horn tips are not cut and capped, making them very dangerous.

A band of trumpets announced the arrival of the *matador* with great fanfare. Bernardo wore blue satin with gold trim, and held a large red and blue cape. His skintight, knee-length breeches and white silk stockings accentuated the highly embroidered short jacket and black shoes. Bernardo's black hair was braided into a plait that hung down his back from under a *montera*, a small black cap. He was the picture of grace.

The first bullfight began. A drum rolled and trumpets blasted as the first black, haughty bull trotted into the plaza looking about in confusion and disdain. Around his neck hung a wreath of flowers representing the colors of his breeder. Señor Medina's wreath is made of yellow daisies and pink roses.

The *picadores*, dressed in black with silver trim, mounted their beautiful horses and jabbed lances at the bull's neck to infuriate him and make him weaker. The raging bull charged at the horses, trying to rip into their withers and flanks. If successful, the horse will die a painful, gruesome death. But the skilled *picadores* steered the horses out of harm's way.

Then came the *banderilleros*, who stick colorful darts into the bull's hump and back. Long bits of colored paper and ribbons stream from the shafts of these picks. They serve to annoy the bull and do not penetrate very deep.

Lastly, the *matador* came, a lonely figure in the center of the plaza who taunted and teased the bull with insulting words and by shaking his bright *capote*. As the angry animal charged, Bernardo skillfully swung the cape and let the bull pass by. The bull learned quickly that there was a man behind the cape and made his charges shorter and shorter. This is when *el toro* is most dangerous, for he can turn and charge the *matador* instead of the cape. Many a man has lost his life this way.

In the cities of Mexico the bull is usually killed by the *matador*'s sword, shoved quickly and mercifully into a small spot behind his neck. Death is instantaneous. If the *matador* has done a good job, he is allowed to take the ear of the bull. The dead bull is slaughtered, and the meat is given to the poor people of the city. But many *rancheros* and *hacienda* owners hold bullfights in which the bulls are not killed.

When the bull is too exhausted to fight anymore, he is lassoed, the darts removed, and ointment applied to his wounds. He will recover and be more fierce for next year's fight.

On the third fight, a bull with his back filled with darts and colorful streamers leaped into the stands. A drummer fell off and broke his arm. Gregorio lassoed the bull, brought him to the ground, then climbed onto his back and rode him around the arena. *Vaqueros* do this often with amazing skill. If the man is thrown, the angry animal will stomp and gore him to death. My heart raced until the bull had finally been roped again and Gregorio dismounted. The *indios* in the trees cheered wildly, for Gregorio is one of their own.

Nelly thought the bullfighting disgusting. It is usually so with *americanos*, but Walter admitted that the men displayed great courage, and as for the bulls, the bullfight gave them a moment of glory and was better than the slaughterhouse.

MAY 14

To my surprise, Rafaela decided to go horseback riding to the hills. She invited Nelly, Walter, and

Gabriela to accompany us. She showed great vigor today, riding her horse with expert skill and climbing up the hill in front of all of us. A stranger who had not seen her since January would have not thought it possible for such a sickly girl to be so healthy and strong now.

The rest of us followed her and scrambled on the rocks. Walter's Spanish is coming along nicely. Nelly and I spoke mostly in English, making Gabriela even more jealous, until she threw down her riding quirt and stomped her foot. "Speak Spanish, Rosa, I order it."

Rafaela heard the command and told Gabriela to leave me alone. She said I was her servant, and could speak English if I wished.

Was this really Rafaela, usually so meek, gentle, and too weak to argue? Gabriela and I exchanged questioning glances. She apologized. I felt badly, too, and began interpreting every word I said to Nelly, so there would be no concern that I was talking about Gabriela behind her back.

May 15

The mystery of Rafaela's transformation is solved. After the Johnstons had left, Rafaela insisted on riding to the hill again. From its top we could see the party riding slowly toward the southwest.

Rafaela exhaled a heavy sigh. "Walter is really a very charming young man," she said. "He is learning Spanish very well. He never looked my way before, but now that I am healthy, he seems very interested. Do you think Papa would approve of another American son-in-law?"

My heart sank. Why, I do not know. After all, why should an American boy as fine as Walter Johnston want to marry a servant girl like me?

I told her I did not know, and my voice was so heavy, I could hardly swallow. The thought of it makes my heart sick, even now.

May 18

An exciting day. All the men were away, except for old Tomás. We were in the courtyard enjoying the pleasant weather. Someone had accidentally left the front gate unlatched. We heard a noise and turned to see a huge grizzly bear lumbering toward Señor Medina's favorite berry vines.

Señora Medina did not hesitate. She ran into the house and came out a moment later with a loaded musket - an old flintlock she inherited from her father. She aimed and fired. Poor Señora Medina fell to the ground, and gunpowder residue covered her fair skin. The bullet missed the target but shattered a pear tree branch that fell smack onto the bear's head. That, along with the roar of the gun, startled him. With a grunt, the grizzly turned and loped out the gate.

MAY 20

A worse day I cannot recall. That grizzly came back. He killed two of the goats, one pig, but worst of all, he wounded one of the servants, leaving a horrible gash across his chest. It was a miracle that he did not die. Señor Medina, Gregorio, and several men decided to hunt the bear down, for once a bear begins to kill livestock, it must be stopped. Of all the animals in California, the grizzly is the one most feared. Its great claws can easily tear a man in half.

Domingo begged to go along, and I was angry that Señor Medina agreed. He said he went on his first bear hunt when he was ten and promised to look after my brother. I know I will not rest until they safely return.

May 23

Three days gone and the men are not back yet. My heart is sick. I cannot stand the thought of losing Domingo. I vow to never be angry with him again.

Sunday, May 24

I did not attend mass, in case Domingo returns. I must be here. Whether to kiss his dirty face or to weep over his mangled body, only God knows.

May 25

¡*Gracias a Dios, Jesús, María, y José!* The men returned, and Domingo was in front singing and laughing. On a litter dragged behind them was the largest grizzly bear I have ever seen. A very old one from the looks of his claws.

I hugged Domingo with all my strength and could not hold back my tears. He excitedly told everyone how he had helped to rope the grizzly, wrap the lariat around a tree, and hold the animal at bay while the men shot it.

The Indian workers are busily skinning the bear now. Señor Medina has given them the meat. Some say it is delicious, but I prefer beef.

May 26

While riding today, Rafaela and I saw more *americano* settlers on Señor Medina's far land. There are three log houses now, with corrals with livestock. Their crops are growing nicely. I served as interpreter for Rafaela. The strangers said they wanted to buy the land. Rafaela explained that if her father sells his land, he'll have no place for his cattle. Domingo said that some of the *americano* cattle belong to the Medina herd. Señor Medina has called a meeting with neighboring *rancheros* over the squatter problem.

MAY 28

Sheepshearing began yesterday. The weather is warmer, and the sheep are ready to shed their thick winter coats. The thought of all the wool that will need to be washed, carded, spun, dyed, and woven into cloth makes me tired.

MAY 30

Sheepshearing has been going for days. The sheep look so skinny and bare when they emerge from the corral, freshly sheared. Domingo is learning how to help hold them down while they are sheared. Professional shearers do the work. They are fast and leave no streaks of red blood from cutting too close. They remove the fleece in one piece, as if the sheep were wearing a wool coat. We washed the fleeces in tubs of soapy water to clean away winter dirt.

SUNDAY, MAY 31

My day of rest. No combing and dyeing the wool today.

JUNE 1

Combing and dyeing. My hands are the colors of the rainbow.

JUNE 2

Started spinning wool into yarn today. Rafaela has the power to rescue me, but she no longer seems interested in riding. She spends her days writing love sonnets and letters to Walter Johnston. I have not seen her send one yet, so I do not think he suspects that he is the object of her aching heart. I know he does not suspect that my own heart aches for him, and he never will know. I could not bear to live if he shunned me.

JUNE 3

Walter Johnston arrived tonight unexpectedly with an urgent message from Yerba Buena. Miguela is feeling poorly. She wants to come home for a while, so that she might be near her mother during this difficult stage of her child-carrying. She will arrive next week. Señora Medina is happy at the news. She misses her daughter terribly.

At the dinner table Walter said that the Americans in Yerba Buena are very mistrustful of the Spanish population. Rumors are running rampant that General Castro, military leader of Alta California, is forming an army and will ride up from Monterey to drive out the Americans, especially those at Sutter's Fort.

Señor Medina snorted and said Castro is too busy bickering with Governor Pío Pico to worry about the Americans. He added that rumors like that only make matters worse among our peoples. "I hope you do not spread such false truths," he said, pointing a fork at Walter.

Walter nodded, but didn't say another word during the meal.

JUNE 4

Walter left before daybreak. I did not even get to say good-bye. Neither did Rafaela. When she heard that he had already left, her eyes filled with tears and she ran to her room and slammed the door. I learned later that she had written him a long, fancy letter and intended to give it to him after breakfast.

JUNE 5

I am sick of looking at wool. Most of it will go for blankets, *rebozos*, and *sarapes*. Some will be spun into thread and woven into cloth.

I have decided to weave a *sarape* for Walter. It will be gray, blue, green, with smaller stripes of yellow and red. I am using the small loom that belonged to Miguela. She rarely used it. I do not know when Walter celebrates his birthday. I must remember to ask Miguela when she arrives. I pray that Nelly will come with her. I miss Nelly so much!

JUNE 6

A party of ten men stopped at the *rancho* today to rest and water their horses. They are under the command of General Castro. They have come all the way from Monterey to Sonoma Valley to obtain horses from General Vallejo, about 160, I think they said.

Señor Medina and two of Castro's lieutenants retired to his office and closed the doors. Their excited, agitated words rose higher and higher as the arguing escalated. I could not hear all their words clearly, but I do know that Señor Medina is very worried and upset.

He said there is already tension between the *californios* and the *americanos* because of rumors. If Castro's men are seen rounding up horses it will look like they are preparing for an armed attack. The *americanos* will no doubt be convinced that Castro's goal is to drive all foreigners from Alta California by force. They will react accordingly.

When the men emerged, Señor Medina's face was red and his eyes were flashing. He quickly ordered his best horse saddled, whispered a few words to his wife, and left, taking Gregorio and two *vaqueros*. I pray that our men will return safely.

SUNDAY, JUNE 7

Lupita begged Señora Medina not to go to Sonoma for mass today, but to no avail. She went not only because it is the celebration of the Holy Trinity but because Señor Johnston and Miguela will be arriving in Sonoma soon.

The Medina women and I rode horses while Domingo, Lupita, and Ramona rode mules packed with baskets of belongings. Rafaela is nervous. She is in great hopes that Walter will accompany Señor Johnston. I am in great hopes that Nelly will come along, too.

Mass was short and afterward people spoke in excited whispers. Rumors fly like crows. Some say that Mexico is at war with the United States. They say the American army has already crossed the Rio Grande in Texas and is fighting on Mexican soil at this very moment. Others say the American army is marching to Alta California and all Mexican citizens will be killed and their lands seized.

The air sings with anticipation. Señora Medina has spent much of the day praying for the safe return of her husband.

JUNE 8

Domingo and other boys are running in the streets playing at war like it is a game. I pray that my dear brother never knows the true nature of war.

Johnston did not arrive today as expected. Señora Medina is almost in hives worried about what may have happened. We are staying at Gertruda's house yet another night. Domingo sleeps in the stable with the horses, which suits him fine. I sleep on the floor with Lupita and Ramona.

It is late now. Many families are loading their belongings in carts and wagons in case they need to get out of Sonoma in a hurry. Señora Medina's sister is a most fearless woman. She loaded two muskets and laid out powder and lead, saying the Americans will take her home only over her dead body.

JUNE 9

Señor Johnston and Miguela arrived today. Miguela had hardly stepped through the door when she vomited into a bucket. Her face is pale, and her clothing smelly. She fell into her mother's arms and wept bitterly while Señor Johnston stood by helplessly wringing his hat. Miguela was immediately put to bed in the guest room. We will have to stay here until she is able to travel.

Miguela is very sick and running a high fever. Señora Medina chastised Señor Johnston fiercely for allowing his wife to get sick in her delicate condition. He muttered and twisted his hat and stumbled outside to get away. I felt sorry for him and followed. He sat on the steps and hung his head low.

I told him that it was not his fault. Women are always a little *loco* when they are with child. He nodded, then smiled and squeezed my hand. "Nelly sends her love," he said. She wanted to come, but she was feeling poorly, too. Johnston supposes it is the same thing that Miguela has. They walked to the docks together a few days ago and encountered a whole family of sick immigrants getting off one of the ships.

"I hope Walter doesn't get sick, too. I'm sure you

need him to watch the store while you're away," I said, trying to sound casual, but I think Johnston saw through me.

Johnston assured me that Walter is fine and healthy. "He sends his best regards to you, Rosa. You know, Walter thinks you're a fine person. And very intelligent."

I didn't hear another word that Johnston said, for my heart was thumping in my chest so loud, I could not even hear my own thoughts.

Johnston decided that his wife is in capable hands, and is returning to Yerba Buena. He said his good-byes and left. I have a strange feeling, but I cannot put it into words. Another night on the floor.

JUNE 10

I saw Lupita crying in the kitchen, her eyes red and her hands shaking. When I asked her what was wrong, she said there is bad trouble. A band of armed ruffian *americanos* attacked Castro's men — the ones who had rounded up the horses from General Vallejo. The *americanos* — mostly trappers dressed in animal hides — accused Castro's men of plotting against them. They warned Castro's men not to attempt to drive immigrants out of Alta California and then stole the herd of horses. Nearly everyone thinks that the American Captain Frémont is behind this. Lupita fears that Frémont will bring his soldiers into Sonoma and burn the town down. But mostly she is afraid that Gregorio and Señor Medina have been hurt.

JUNE 11

Miguela's condition is worse. The older women say her illness has nothing to do with being with child. It is something much more sinister. Lupita's eyes are full of worry. She will not let me or the Medina daughters or Domingo near Miguela's room. Gabriela whispered into my ear "cholera," but she does not know that for sure. If so, we are all doomed, for it is a horrible and contagious disease that often destroys entire villages and towns. We three girls walked to the chapel and prayed for an hour and burned candles for Miguela. I also burned one for Nelly.

JUNE 12

The household was awakened by loud shrieks this morning just before dawn. We girls ran into the hall, our long night dresses flowing, our long hair flying behind us. Lupita met us outside Miguela's closed door and pushed us back. She instructed me to go into the kitchen and start a pot of coffee, and told the sisters to go back to bed.

"You can do nothing here. Miguela miscarried the child."

"And what of my sister?" Rafaela asked, her face white as a shroud.

"She is strong and will survive. It will take more than a wicked disease to kill Miguela. Now go. . . ."

I went to the kitchen, and the two sisters followed me. As I made coffee and prepared *tortillas*, they clung to each other, weeping for the lost babe.

This afternoon we went to church to pray for the soul of the unborn infant. Later, the priest wrapped its remains in satin and lace and placed it in a tiny wooden box for burial. Now I am sick with worry for Nelly and Walter, and even Señor Johnston himself.

June 13

The women all wore black today in honor of the dead baby. Miguela's fever broke, and Lupita is sure she will recover soon. We hope to return home in two or three days. It will be good to get away from this dark house of death.

Sunday, June 14

It is almost dawn. The household is in a deep sleep, but I am restless. I hear dogs barking at General Vallejo's house across the town plaza. I hear men's voices and the whinny of horses. Something is going on. Domingo was awakened by the noise, too, and crawled over to the window beside me.

"*¿Qué pasa?*" he asked me, rubbing his sleepy eyes and peering into the darkness. We saw candlelight flicker in Vallejo's front windows.

"I do not know, little brother, but men who sneak about in the darkness cannot be up to anything good."

I must stop writing and go tell Lupita.

LATER IN THE DAY

All of Sonoma is stunned. The noises I heard this morning were Americans. Mostly rough trappers in buckskin and animal hides — the same ones who attacked Castro's men and stole their horses. There are about thirty of them armed with rifles, pistols, and knives. They have gathered outside General Vallejo's house demanding his arrest. Vallejo sent for his brother-in-law, Jacob Leese, who speaks both Spanish and English, to serve as an interpreter. Now General Vallejo, his brother Salvador, his secretary Señor Prudon, and Jacob Leese are inside discussing terms with the man chosen to represent the disgruntled Americans.

The town is anxiously waiting to hear what is happening. No one dares to approach the unruly *americanos,* who sit about grumbling. They appear to be a very impatient bunch.

I noticed Señora Medina getting dressed for mass. Lupita said, "Señora, *por favor,* you cannot go to church today. The town is being besieged. It is too dangerous out there."

But the señora ignored her and said, "Lupita, I just

buried my first grandchild. Nothing the *americanos* do can pain my heart more than that."

Doña Gertruda took inspiration from her sister and dressed her own children for mass. We walked across the plaza to the adobe church attached to Solano Mission. Many people stayed home, and those who came glanced over their shoulders nervously at the band of rough-clad Americans outside General Vallejo's house. They were now eating. The general had given instructions that a bullock be killed, and the food was distributed to the Americans. Even in times of crisis, Spanish hospitality cannot be forsaken.

By mid-morning we had returned to the house, but we children could not sit still. We climbed the court-yard wall and watched the greasy men as they ate and grumbled among themselves. Apparently they were very impatient for the meeting inside the general's house to be over.

Around eleven o'clock, the general emerged, immaculately dressed, accompanied by his brother-in-law, his secretary, and his brother. Though they did not struggle, it was obvious that the Vallejo party was under arrest. As the small party of prisoners and their captors rode by the house, the general held his head high. A wave of pride roared through my veins. Domingo stood on the wall and saluted like a soldier. Never have I seen the general with such a look of sadness on his handsome face. His wife and children and sister stood nearby, tears in their eyes, but with their chins held up. My heart ached for the family that had almost single-handedly built the Sonoma Valley into the prosperous patchwork of *ranchos*.

The Americans who stayed behind quickly informed the priest and the *alcalde* that Sonoma was now under their rule. They loudly proclaimed California's independence from Mexico and the birth of the Republic of California. Some Americans took a piece of white muslin from a servant woman and made a crude flag. They painted a single red star in the left corner and a very sickly looking bear in the other. At the bottom of the flag they stitched a strip of red petticoat and the words REPUBLIC OF CALIFORNIA.

The flag of Mexico was hauled down from the pole in the plaza near the old barracks, and this new Bear Flag was hoisted in its place. My heart feels very strange. I am thankful there was no bloodshed, and General Vallejo's parting words told us not to worry for he was in safe hands, but still I do not feel like I am now in a new country. Nothing has changed except for the hungry *americano* trappers who walk the streets with their muskets and huge hunting knives.

Tonight I lit a candle for General Vallejo and his family.

JUNE 15

There is still much confusion in the town. Everyone wonders if California is a free republic or now part of America. A messenger arrived this afternoon, saying that General Vallejo's party was being taken to Captain Frémont, who is camped on the American River.

Everyone is now calling the band of Americans *Osos* — Bears — because of the flag. Their leader is a man named William B. Ide. Today he read a proclamation and posted it. Townspeople have been talking about it all day.

Miguela is regaining her strength, so Señora Medina wants to return to Rancho Agua Verde tomorrow. She is eager to find out if Señor Medina is back. We have not heard from him since June 6 when he left with Gregorio. Señora Medina is deeply worried, for it is not like her husband to not send word.

JUNE 16

Señora Medina tried to leave today, but the Osos would not let us. They say that no one can leave or enter the town without their permission. Señora Medina is furious. We returned to the house and unpacked the mules. Miguela is worried about Señor Johnston. Three days ago she sent a messenger to Yerba Buena with word of her miscarriage. She is afraid he will try to come into town and be arrested if he causes a stir.

JUNE 17

Several women walked to General Vallejo's house. The Osos guarding it let us pass. Señora Vallejo is presenting a brave front. She had received word that her husband was now a prisoner at Sutter's Fort, escorted there by Kit Carson, a famous American scout.

The general is being fed and treated well by Sutter. Señora Vallejo was preparing a package for the general, including personal supplies, books, and his beautiful chess set — the finest in California.

I touched the piano. It feels like polished black stone, but warm. The Vallejo house is a miracle of fine furniture, paintings, tapestries, and rugs. But the children are sad that their father is a prisoner. At this moment, I would not want to trade places with them at all.

JUNE 19

Miguela received the most heart-wrenching letter from Johnston expressing his grief over the loss of their unborn child. He said he tried to get into Sonoma but was turned away. He is now working through the *alcalde* to get permission to bring Miguela home to Yerba Buena.

JUNE 20

Today is the celebration of the Immaculate Heart of Mary; yesterday was the Sacred Heart of Jesus. Señora

Medina and her sister attended mass and pretended that all is well. Miguela is fully recovered, so she walked with her mother to the mission church. Some American ruffians saw her and made improper advances. She poked one with her parasol point. He doubled over, and his friends laughed hysterically. When he tried to grab her again, Rafaela came to her sister's rescue and kicked the man on his shin. Then we all ran.

During mass, all I could think about was the Osos waiting outside the doors to grab us, but they were gone when we got out. I guess the priest's long-winded mass was too much for them to endure. Señora Medina said we girls cannot go outside the house without chaperons.

June 22

I feel like a prisoner in this house! The only fresh air we get is in the courtyard, or when we go to the well for water. Only Domingo is allowed to roam about as he pleases. He and the other boys are curious about the shaggy Osos and pester them constantly. The Americans do not seem to care that boys are tagging after them. I do not think any of the Osos speak Spanish.

JUNE 24

Today is Señora Medina's saint's day. She was cheered momentarily when Gertruda baked delicious *pan dulce* and gave her sister a set of pearls that had belonged to their mother. The señora smiled for the first time in many days.

JUNE 25

We are more worried than ever about Señor Medina. Today we received word that a battle took place near San Rafael yesterday. Fifty *californios* sent by Castro were met by *americanos* near a place called Olompali. Two *americanos* and six *californios* were killed. Though we tell her not to worry, Señora Medina is convinced that her husband was among them. She has been praying all day.

June 26

Gabriela, Rafaela, and I, and even Miguela have been playing games in the courtyard like little children — tossing stones, making bridges with our hands, and singing, all to pass the time of day. We want to go home so bad we could scream.

Sunday, June 28

Thank goodness the señora decided to attend mass today, in spite of last week's encounter with the Osos. The walk was uneventful, except that I saw the blacksmith's assistant, Pedro, limping down the street, using a cedar stick as a crutch. I asked him what had happened, and he said an Oso had tripped him as he ran, after stealing a piece of jerked beef. He was starving now because the blacksmith was punishing Pedro by withholding his meager food. I felt so sorry for Pedro, I gave him the coin I had planned to place in the church offering box. I think God would prefer that the money be spent this way.

June 29

Word has slipped through to us about a dreadful event. Yesterday Captain Frémont and his men murdered an old man by the name of Berryessa, as well as twin brothers with him named de Haro. They were innocently rowing in a boat and unarmed. There is no excuse for this and citizens are more convinced than ever that Frémont is a cold-hearted monster. I dread the day that he arrives in Sonoma, but it is inevitable.

June 30

At last Señor Johnston was allowed to come into Sonoma and retrieve Miguela. They hugged, and you never would have known that a few months ago Miguela was calling him names and wishing he would go away. I could not help but smile at the change in her. She is almost as nice as Rafaela now, except for an occasional burst of temper.

Johnston took me aside while Miguela was packing. He gave me a little gold locket. It was the one that I had admired around Nelly's neck many times.

"Rosa," he said, making me sit down. "Nelly wanted you to have this, to remember her by."

I saw big tears form in his blue eyes, and suddenly my heart sank to my feet. He swallowed hard, his Adam's apple bobbing up and down.

"Dear, sweet Nelly passed away a few days after I returned to Yerba Buena. She caught the disease from that cursed ship. Several people died. I thank God that my Miguela and Walter survived."

I took the locket in my shaking fingers and felt the hot tears sliding down my cheeks. I could not speak. Johnston nodded and held me in his strong arms. "I know, I know," he whispered, patting my back. Then he slipped the locket around my neck. "Think of her every time you see this locket. That way she will live on in your heart forever."

I am looking at the locket now as I write. Tears are blurring the words. Nelly was such a dear, sweet girl. I know she is in Heaven with her family.

JULY 2

Señor Johnston and Miguela left today. Miguela was so happy to be with her husband, but at the same time I know she was worried about the rest of us. Señora Medina has implored the *alcalde* to act on her behalf and convince the Osos to let us return to the *rancho*. We are so worried about Señor Medina.

JULY 4

Today is the celebration of America's Independence. The Osos shot off guns, drank, and made speeches. This night there were a few fireworks. I am so proud of Domingo. Even though he loves fireworks dearly, he refused to participate, out of loyalty to Mother Mexico. He will make a fine man one day.

Frémont and about ninety American soldiers arrived in time for the celebration. He is a haughty man, who struts about like he owns Sonoma, though he had no part in its capture. I think Ide, leader of the Osos, is not very happy to see Frémont. I would love to see them at each other's throats.

SUNDAY, JULY 5

After mass, the women visited Señora Vallejo again. She was preparing some special foods and gifts, for Tuesday is the general's birthday. He will be thirty-eight years old. He has accomplished more in his lifetime than most men accomplish in fifty years. We sang some cheerful songs, and the oldest daughter played the piano. It felt like a party, though the guest of honor was not there.

JULY 7

At last we received word that Señor Medina is fine. He had fallen from his horse and broken his leg, making it impossible for him to travel. Indians cared for him for three weeks. He is now back at the *rancho* and recovering nicely. He begged his wife's forgiveness for not letting her know sooner. He was shocked to find out that she was in Sonoma and that Vallejo was a prisoner. He said he would make arrangements for us to come back to the *rancho* very soon. We all shouted as if it were a *fiesta*, and Domingo stood on his head, making us laugh. We are delirious with relief.

July 9

We are packing and preparing to leave. Gregorio arrived late this evening with the *carreta*, pulled by two
strong oxen. Lupita hugged him until he almost
turned purple. Then she chased him with a broom for
taking so long to get here.

I am so happy to be returning to the *rancho*. Words
cannot describe the joy, the relief, the hope. I pray
that the Osos will not change their minds and stop us
from leaving.

July 10

The infant Republic of California is no more. Today,
while we were preparing to leave for the *rancho*, a
man rode into the plaza. I learned later that his name
was Lieutenant Revere. He is related to the famous
Paul Revere, who was a hero of the American
Revolution. Lieutenant Revere announced that the
United States and Mexico had been at war since May
13, and that American warships had landed at
Monterey, the military capital of California, on July
7. Monterey was taken without a shot being fired, and

the American flag was raised. On July 9, an American warship landed at Yerba Buena and raised the American flag there, again without a shot being fired.

Today, Lieutenant Revere lowered the Bear Flag, and raised in its place the stars and stripes of the American flag. As of this moment, the United States of America claims Alta California as her own. The Osos cheered, though a few of them seemed disappointed.

Gregorio shook his head as we climbed into the cart. "This is the end of California," he said softly. "The end of the valley of the moon. There will be no more peace for *californios* from this day forth."

We rode in silence back to the *rancho*. A messenger on horseback passed us. He was carrying another American flag to be raised over Sutter's Fort. I wonder what the plump Swiss businessman will say about that?

Domingo was upset. He thinks the *californios* should fight the *americanos*, but Gregorio is more practical. He says there is no point. If Mexico wins the war, perhaps we will be returned to her, but in truth Mexico does not care about Alta California. We are too remote, and Mexico has too many problems of her own.

Gregorio thinks it is only a matter of time until California becomes another state in the Union, just like Texas. We will have American governors, American laws, American churches and schools. More American settlers will come.

And what about the *californios*? What will become of us? I wonder. Will we disappear into the pages of history? Will our language, our customs, our *ranchos* — everything we hold dear — vanish like a fleeting rainbow? The thought of it saddens my heart beyond words. I cannot write anymore tonight.

JULY 11

We arrived back at Rancho Agua Verde late in the afternoon. Never did the old adobe walls look so welcoming. Señor Medina was standing at the front door leaning on a heavy oak stick, his leg wrapped in bandages. His daughters leaped from the cart and flew to his side, smothering him with hugs and kisses. I felt a twinge of jealousy as never before. I wanted to welcome him back, too, but Domingo and I simply stood by with Lupita and Gregorio, our hands by our sides.

When at last the family had gone inside, Señor Medina turned and looked at me and Domingo. He smiled and welcomed us back. He told Lupita that she had lost weight. She giggled and said she knew how to fix that and left for the kitchen.

"*¡Bueno!*" the señor said with gusto, then went inside. The door closed behind him. I do not know why my heart is so heavy tonight. Is it because California is under siege by the Americans? Or is it because Señor Medina's affection for his children only reminds me again that I have no father?

As I prepared for bed, I looked at the vaccination scar on my arm. Someone had cared enough to save my life. Someone had cared enough to take me and Domingo to the mission. Someone must have loved us. But who? Why did my father not return to the mission and take us home to live with him? Did he have a Spanish wife and children already? Did he die? Why do these thoughts torment me? So many years have gone by, what difference does it make now?

SUNDAY, JULY 12

I did not sleep last night. I tossed with fitful dreams — images of a tall, strong man hugging me and Domingo close. He had a small mustache and a handsome face. My mother stood quietly on the steps of an adobe house, holding the reins of a fine white horse. Her eyes were sad and full of tears.

"*Adiós*, my children," he said to me and Domingo.

When I awakened, I jumped up and ran to Domingo's room. I shook him until he woke with a grunt and whimper. I asked him if he had ever dreamed about a Spaniard hugging us in his arms.

Domingo rubbed his eyes, then opened them wide. "You mean the tall man with the mustache?"

I asked him if our mother was on the steps of a house, holding the reins of a beautiful white horse. Domingo nodded and exclaimed, "How do you know about my dreams, sister?"

I put my hands over my mouth to muffle the gasp. "Because it was not a dream, little brother."

I told him to go back to sleep. My life has purpose now. I know there is hope. And I know that only one man can tell me the truth — Padre Ygnacio.

JULY 13

I helped Lupita and Ramona with chores all day. The work had piled up while we were in Sonoma. Every chance I got, I slipped in a question about Padre Ygnacio, or about my mother or my father. It is clear to me that Lupita knows nothing of my past or of the padre's whereabouts. Perhaps Gregorio knows more. I will speak to him first chance I get.

July 14

Early this morning I hurried to the corral to find Gregorio. He was showing Domingo how to tie his lariat into a complicated knot to keep the horses together in a string. I must admit, Domingo is very talented and patient when it comes to ropes and cows. There is no doubt that he will make a fine *vaquero*. They were surprised to see me at the corral.

I handed Gregorio a mug of steaming coffee. It was my excuse to be there. He said, *"Gracias, Señorita,"* but looked at me with suspicious eyes.

I glanced at Domingo, who was as curious as Gregorio, took a deep breath, and asked Gregorio if he remembered Padre Ygnacio. Gregorio took a long sip of coffee and stared at the horizon a long time, then nodded. *"Sí.* I met the old priest a few times. Why do you ask?"

I swallowed hard. "I must talk to him about my mother. Do you know where he is now?"

Gregorio screwed his eyebrows and frowned. He took another long sip of coffee, then tossed the contents of the cup to the ground. "No," he said abruptly. "No one knows. You'd better get back to the kitchen." He turned his back, picked up the rope, and began twirling it furiously.

There is no doubt in my mind now that the only way I will find the answers to my questions is to find Padre Ygnacio himself. But where do I begin?

JULY 16

This afternoon, after *siesta*, I summoned every ounce of courage in my body and approached Señora Medina, tiptoeing in to the family *sala*, where she and Rafaela were busily embroidering a lovely tablecloth. The flowers and birds vibrated with colors. Gabriela was helping them, but without much enthusiasm.

I swallowed hard, took a deep breath, then asked permission to go to Mission Rafael again to find out what happened to Padre Ygnacio.

The señora's face turned pale a moment, then she picked up the needle again. "I heard a rumor that Padre Ygnacio left the priesthood. And good riddance. Many thought him a heretic. He read far too many un-Christian books."

"But I must find out where he is. He is the only one who might know about my parents."

"Rosalia! You must get the idea of finding Padre Ygnacio out of your head. The priest at Mission Rafael might know his whereabouts, but it is impossible for you to go at this time. Don't you know there's a war going on?"

Gabriela sat up, her eyes twinkling. After I'd been dismissed, Gabriela caught up with me in the grand corridor. She told me that her mother was planning on sending Gregorio to Yerba Buena this Sunday with some things for Miguela. I thanked her for that bit of information, but I knew it was pointless to bother Señora Medina again. Her mind was obviously made up.

Well, my mind is made up, too. I have been thinking all day, and I know what I must do.

❧ ❧

July 18

My plan begins. I have packed some food and extra clothing into a bag. And, of course, my diary — my most precious possession. I will hide it under my petticoat tomorrow when we go to mass.

Sunday, July 19

We attended mass in Sonoma. Captain Frémont, his army, and the Osos have all left. The *americanos* are marching to Monterey looking for any *californios* who might want to fight. I am glad they have left. I do not want to worry about *americanos* on my journey.

During mass, I snuck out and ran to the stables where Gergorio was preparing to leave for Yerba Buena. He was loading a pack mule with items for Miguela. When he saw my bundle, he thought I was adding something to the other packages. May God forgive me for telling him a lie.

I told him that Señora Medina wanted me to accompany him to see if Miguela needed help. I thought I was convincing, but Gregorio looked doubtful.

"The señora did not tell me such a thing," he said.

"She only just now made the decision" I said. "I will be no trouble. I will walk behind the mule."

Perhaps it was the desperate look on my face, but he finally sighed and looked at the church. I know he was debating whether he should wait for mass to end and get a late start, or take a chance that I was telling the truth. Suddenly, he saw the blacksmith's assistant and called him over with a loud, "¡Muchacho!"

Gregorio told Pedro to run into the church and ask Señora Medina if what I had said was true. He even promised the boy a *centavo* if he would hurry. Pedro ran on his skinny legs, his rags flying in the breeze. He slipped into the church, and a moment later ran back, gasping for air. My heart pounded as he huffed before finally speaking.

"It's all right, Señor. The lady says Rosa may go." He held out his hand and received a dull copper coin. I thanked him with my eyes, and he nodded.

All along the way we passed Mexican families in wagons loaded with their belongings. Many said they were going back to Mexico, or to remote *ranchos* where the *americanos* would not find them. *Rancheros* were boarding up their doors and shutters to keep the rough Osos out. Gregorio assures me that the *americanos* have already passed by on their way to

Monterey, but still I keep glancing over my shoulder at every little noise in the woods or grass.

We arrived safely at Mission Rafael. It is too dark to cross San Francisco Bay now, so we stay here. My plan is working like a miracle so far. The priest is asleep, but tomorrow I shall try to learn the fate of Padre Ygnacio.

JULY 20

The priest was up before daylight preparing for matins. The church bell pealed at seven o'clock, drawing in a few local *californios* and some devoted Indians, who knelt on the cold stone floor. Afterward, I asked the priest what had happened to Padre Ygnacio. Like everyone else, he did not want to discuss the fate of my old friend. But at last he said:

"Padre Ygnacio left the mission three years ago. Rumor has it that he has forsaken his vows and taken an Indian wife. He lives outside Monterey."

This was a shock to me, for the good padre seemed so devoted to the Church. I learned his surname for the first time — Morales.

I crossed San Francisco Bay with Gregorio and the packages. As usual, fog swirled and cold water sent chills up my spine when it sloshed into the boat. I helped Gregorio carry the goods to the Johnstons' house. Miguela was completely surprised at our arrival and pleased beyond words that I had accompanied Gregorio. She raved about how thoughtful it was of her mother to send a servant to take care of the house, which apparently had not been cleaned since Nelly's death. She expressed the desire that I should stay for at least a month, claiming that she was still feeling poorly. But from the looks of her hips, I would say that she certainly has not lost her appetite.

I dared not refuse, so I set about cleaning the house, washing clothes, and helping the cook, who refused to do the heavy work. I was glad to have something to take my mind off Padre Ygnacio.

Late in the afternoon, Walter Johnston came in. My face turned every shade of red when I bumped into him in the hall, my arms full of freshly washed linens. He grinned, removed his hat, and apologized for being so dirty. He had been at the docks all day unloading goods off a ship. He is as pleased as a possum that the Americans have "rescued" California, as he words it. He had cheered Captain Frémont on July 2, when they took Yerba Buena.

"And just whom did the Americans rescue California from?" I asked. My voice was not very sweet. He seemed taken aback by the question, for he thought a long time before replying.

"Well, I guess we've rescued California from you Spanish, just the way the Spanish rescued California from the Indians." With that he crammed his hat on his head and left. If I were a man, I would have punched him in his face, but all I could do was stomp my foot and huff. Maybe I won't enjoy my stay here after all.

July 21

I am swamped with chores. Every time I finish one, Miguela finds another. The cook is no help at all. She is shiftless and lazy and finds most ingenious ways of sneaking out of the house when it is time to work.

I think Walter regrets being rude to me. He showed me Nelly's grave, a pretty spot near a tree in the cemetery of nearby Mission Dolores. I wept and placed flowers on her grave. Walter removed his hat and hung his head. He fought back the tears, but I know his heart was aching. All his family is gone now except for Señor Johnston. I wanted to hold Walter's hand and tell him I knew what it was like to be an orphan, but I was afraid he would not want it.

July 22

Gregorio says he must return to Rancho Agua Verde. Miguela begged me to stay and be her permanent servant. She says she will get it approved by her mother. I told her I would have to return to the *rancho* first. I pray that the señora will ignore Miguela's pleas, but I am sure to be punished for running away and lying. What better punishment than making me serve Miguela?

July 23

I heard Walter saying that he is going by ship to Monterey to supervise the purchase and loading of important goods. I wish I could stow away and go with him, but it is out of the question. I have strayed too far from grace already and vow to never lie or deceive again.

Before leaving, I handed Walter a letter for Padre Ygnacio and told him all I knew about the old man's whereabouts. Walter said he would do his best to deliver it. A perfect gentleman, he did not ask what was in the letter. He took my hand and kissed it gently. How I wanted to throw my arms around his neck and hug him with all my might, but instead I curtsied and said, *"Vaya con Dios."*

JULY 25

I am back at the *rancho*. Señora Medina was angry at first, but when she learned that I had helped Miguela and that Miguela wanted me to be her servant, the señora's heart softened and she forgave my excursion. Gabriela and Rafaela gave me warm, welcoming hugs. Domingo merely shrugged and said, "So, you're back." I will wait until another day to explain to him why I went.

Sunday, July 26

Rafaela allowed me to stay home while everyone is at mass. Señor Medina stayed home, too. His broken bone is mending, but he walks with a slight limp, and I know he feels pain from time to time.

About mid-morning, Señor Medina called me into his library and asked me if I had found Padre Ygnacio. He said this casually, not bothering to look up from his massive oak desk.

"No, Señor. Padre Ygnacio is gone."

"Lupita told me that you are trying to find out who your mother and father were. Don't you think that the good padre would have told you anything he knew?" Señor Medina put down his ink quill, and his eyes grew dark.

I shrugged. "Perhaps he did not know at the time. Or perhaps someone ordered him not to tell me."

Señor Medina finished writing his letter, then dropped hot wax on the crease. He pressed his signet ring into the warm liquid, leaving a perfect "M" imprinted on the seal. "Now, Rosa, who would order a priest about?"

"Someone with authority and influence," I said.

Señor Medina did not mince words. He told me to drop my foolish quest. He said that Padre Ygnacio was mentally unbalanced; that the old man made up strange stories and saw ghosts. Some say he was only spared from excommunication by agreeing to leave the Church.

I felt my chin begin to quiver as I hurried away from Señor Medina and his dark eyes. It wasn't true. Padre Ygnacio was kind and intelligent. He often got into trouble with his superiors because he read liberal books. If he had been excommunicated, it was because he had dared to challenge the Church, not because he was insane. I feel closer to the old priest now than ever before.

JULY 27

This morning Rafaela and Señora Medina called me into the family *sala*. In her hand the señora was holding Miguela's letter requesting me to go to Yerba Buena and become her servant. Rafaela said she did not mind.

"What about Domingo?" I asked. "May he come with me?"

"He is needed here. He will make a fine *vaquero*, and Gregorio loves him like a son. Señor Medina is very fond of him, too, you know. In many ways Domingo is like the son we never had. We will make sure he continues his studies."

Señora Medina told me I did not have to go if I did not want to. I have a few days to think it over.

As I walked down the long corridor lined with paintings of deceased Medinas, I felt numb all over. If the Medinas loved Domingo so dearly and did not want him to leave, didn't it stand to reason that they did not care for me at all, since they were willing to let me go? With a heavy heart I returned to my chores, but I could not concentrate.

JULY 29

I gave Señora Medina my decision today. I will go to live with the Johnstons. Ramona was kind enough to say she would miss me terribly, and Gabriela threw a fit at the news. Domingo pretends he does not care, but he is not speaking to me. How I wish I could take him with me, but he is far better off here, where he is loved and wanted. He will get an education and perhaps become the son Señor Medina never had. If he came with me, he would run wild in the streets and probably become a soldier at the *presidio*.

AUGUST 1

All my possessions fit into one cloth bag. Gregorio is to escort me to Yerba Buena after mass tomorrow. My heart is torn in two.

SUNDAY, AUGUST 2

In Sonoma, mass was interrupted by word that General Vallejo had just arrived back home after all this time in prison at Fort Sutter. He is weak from suffering a case of malaria. Domingo and I stood on Doña Gertruda's wall looking into the courtyard of the Vallejo mansion. We saw the general, weak and shaky, come outside and start a bonfire. He returned in a few moments with garments colored blue and red. He tossed them onto the fire.

"It is his general's uniform!" Domingo exclaimed.

We stood with mouths agape as the general burned

all his beautiful Mexican uniforms. Domingo did not understand how the general could do such a thing, but I knew it meant that he no longer gave his allegiance to Mexico.

"California is no longer part of Mexico," I said. "We belong to America now."

Domingo climbed down and kicked the dirt. "I'm not an *americano!* I've heard that the *californios* in the south are raising an army to fight the *americanos*. If I were only a couple of years older, I'd join them."

I ruffled his hair, then pulled him close and buried my face in his *sarape* that smelled of horses and grease. "I love you, little brother. You must promise to come see me sometime in Yerba Buena. And I'll visit you every time the Johnstons come to the *rancho*."

Domingo looked up, and water glistened in his dark eyes when he asked me why I must go. I tried to make him understand that I had to find out who our parents were, but Domingo said he did not care. He does not remember our mother. Lupita and Gregorio are his mama and papa.

Later, I said good-bye to Gabriela and Rafaela and Lupita. Even Señora and Señor Medina gave me a hug and brief kiss, as if they truly would miss me. As I climbed on the horse, I wondered if maybe Domingo was right. Maybe I should just forget our mother and father and accept my life as it is.

AUGUST 4

Arrived at Yerba Buena without incident. There was a ship in the harbor named *Brooklyn*. It carried a load of *americanos* who call themselves Mormons. They looked poorly from the long trip.

AUGUST 5

Gregorio left today. I said good-bye to him with such a lump in my throat that I could not speak. At last he smiled and said:

"Come home anytime, little angel. You are always welcome to live with Lupita and me. We think of you as our daughter, you know. Whatever it is you are seeking, may you find it and have peace." With that he placed a sweet kiss on my cheek, then put on his sweat-stained hat and climbed aboard the ferry. My heart was so heavy, I could not breathe.

Miguela put me to work the moment I stepped inside the Johnston house. I did not have time to think about much else all day. The cook is as plain as a river stone and prepares the most boring of foods. Miguela has instructed me to teach Cook some new dishes.

Walter devoured my cooking, though in my opinion the dishes are not half as good as Lupita's. I suppose anything would taste good compared with the gruel that the cook has been dishing out to the unfortunate Johnston family.

I have been trying to summon the courage to speak to Walter, who returned from Monterey just yesterday. He has been at the docks or working in the store most of the time. He is full of excitement over the goings-on of this so-called war. Captain Frémont and the Osos arrived in Monterey while Walter was there, but soon left, heading south for Los Angeles, planting American flags along the way. They have met little resistance from the *californios* living in northern California. I think most people do not care who rules California, as long as they are left to mind their own *ranchos* and farms. The southern *californios* are expected to put up a fight.

Señor Johnston had a thin American newspaper and read it cover to cover, then let me have it. It is full of news of the war raging between Mexico and the United States. All the major battles are occurring in Mexico. General Santa Anna leads the Mexican army, while Zachary Taylor leads the American troops. The newspaper said that over one hundred thousand Americans, mostly Texans, marched with Taylor across the Rio Grande.

Walter seems very disappointed that there is not more fighting and bloodshed here in northern California. He asked Señor Johnston if he might join Frémont's troops and go south, but Johnston said no in such a loud, firm voice that it is clear he does not want any part of this war. I must wait for the appropriate moment to ask Walter if he found Padre Ygnacio.

August 6

Today, while most of the household was taking *siesta*, I was picking beans from the garden, when I heard footsteps behind me. I turned and saw Walter approaching. My heart was like thunder in my chest. He knelt down beside me and began picking beans and putting them in the basket.

"I almost forgot to tell you about Padre Ygnacio,"

he said casually. "He gave me a letter to deliver to you." He withdrew a crumpled, stained pack of sheaves folded many times. "Sorry it's such a mess. Guess I forgot it was in my pocket. But I didn't read it."

My hands began trembling so that I dropped a bean pod. I took the letter from Walter's hands and felt its lightness. My future hinged on these thin leaves of paper. I could not breathe and had to force myself to speak again.

When I asked if the padre was in good health, Walter shook his head sadly. The padre is very old. He is living in a run-down adobe house on the edge of the woods, surrounded by wildflowers and a big garden. He has two Indian servants waiting on him. As far as Walter could tell, the padre doesn't work for the Church anymore. He can hardly walk, from rickety bones. His hands are all twisted, and he is in constant pain. The padre knows he only has a little while to live.

Walter rose and replaced his hat. "I sure hope that letter has good news for you, Rosa. You deserve something good to happen."

With that, he left me alone with the letter. I could not bring myself to read it at that moment. It is now past midnight, and the house is asleep. I will open it as soon as I say my prayers.

August 7

My heart is in my throat as I write. How my life has suddenly changed. At first I could not read Padre Ygnacio's handwriting. His hands must be in great pain, for his script was wobbly and the letters ran together. But after much struggle, at last I deciphered the words. I will record them here as a memento for my grandchildren to read, for it concerns their heritage:

My dearest María Rosalia —

God's blessing upon you. I was so touched to hear from you and to learn that you and Domingo are doing well. How proud of you I am! You turned into a fine young woman, according to the messenger.

To answer your questions, I must first inform you that I am in poorest of health and will soon cast off this mortal coil. It is for this reason that I feel I must tell you the circumstances of your mother's death. I learned of your birthright in bits and pieces over the years. When the truth was finally revealed, I was sworn to secrecy by a man who had the power to destroy me, but that matters not now.

Your mother belonged to a people who live far to the south. I'm told she was beautiful, kind, gentle, and full of life. The daughter of the tribal shaman, she was following in his footsteps and was learning the cures of herbs and roots when the Mexican government forced her village to relocate. A handsome young captain who was in charge of moving the people fell under the spell of her beauty and charm. He loved her, I have no doubt, but he could not marry an Indian — his family, all *criollos* descended from pure Spanish blood, was too wealthy and important. The couple went through a native marriage ceremony performed by her father. When the young captain was transferred to the *presidio* at San Francisco Bay in 1836, he brought your mother with him. He built a small house for her and their little daughter. A son was born that year.

The captain was away in Mexico on army business when the horrible smallpox plague broke out. Soldiers and Mexican settlers were vaccinated, but the Indians were unprotected and died in great numbers. Your mother saw that the traditional cures of her people were useless against the white man's disease, so she went to

Mission Dolores for medicine. She was told there was only enough vaccine left for two people. Like any good mother, she made the ultimate sacrifice and gave the vaccine to her children, taking none for herself.

She hoped that there was vaccine at Mission Rafael across the bay, but the ferryman would not take her across for fear of her disease. She had to wait for days until she found an abandoned raft and took it across by herself. By the time she reached Mission Rafael, she was too far gone to save. I did not know who she was at that time and began raising you and Domingo as orphans.

When the captain finally returned to *Presidio de San Francisco* almost a year later, he found his little house empty. People told him his family had died in the plague. He had no reason to doubt it. After his tour ended at the *presidio*, he moved to Monterey and was promoted to a significant position. He never married and died young, some say because of the sorrow he always carried.

I pray that you will forgive me, an old, dying man, for my selfish acts. When I found you children, your dear mother was dying. She was whispering "padre" to me as she pointed to her finger. Upon it was a lovely golden signet ring. She was too weak to take it from her finger, so I did so for her. She pointed to it, whispered "padre" again, then died.

I thought she was telling me, the padre, to keep the ring — perhaps as a reward for taking her children. It fit my small finger perfectly, and I grew very fond of it. I used it as my own signet ring when I sent letters to friends. When you moved to the Medina *rancho*, I should have given you the ring, but I was selfish. I had worn it for four years and had come to think of it as my own.

About a year after you and Domingo left, I sent a letter to Señor Medina and used the signet in the letter's wax seal. Señor Villareal, the *mayordomo* for the Medina *rancho*, saw the signet and intercepted the letter. He paid me a visit and informed that the ring belonged to Antonio Medina, the younger brother of Señor Medina. Villareal threatened to reveal to the bishop in Mexico City that I read certain forbidden works of liberal thinkers and was too liberal with the Church's money in helping the local Indians. It would have meant excommunication and the damnation of my soul. I left Mission Rafael to avoid that fate. Villareal promised that you and Domingo would be well taken care of. I always meant to return the ring. Please take it now and give this letter to Señor

Medina, your uncle. I know he will do the right thing. Forgive me, my child, and may the love of *Jesucristo* protect you. Forever your devoted servant,

Padre Ygnacio Juan Morales

My heart is singing and weeping at the same time as I hold the golden ring with the letter "M" on it. It looks exactly like the ring that Señor Medina wears, and exactly like the ring in the portrait of Antonio Medina hanging in the corridor: a handsome man with a small mustache, the same man who appeared in my dreams. I am too exhausted to write my feelings tonight. I will return to my diary when my thoughts are in order. I am afraid of the future. So afraid.

THREE MONTHS LATER— NOVEMBER 2, 1846

El Día de los Muertos has arrived again. Today I visited the grave of my mother. I spread marigolds over the ground and lit candles. Pink roses cascade over the new tombstone that I had erected for her. I am writing her a letter. I will tear it out of the diary and place it under a stone. It is all I can do.

My letter to Mamá:

Beloved mother,

At last I know who you are. Padre Ygnacio solved the mystery of your identity. And I know who my papa was, too. Domingo and I are well. Domingo has grown an inch this year. He is wearing fine clothes now, a gift of Señor Medina, when he learned that Domingo was his nephew. Walter Johnston was kind enough to accompany me to Rancho Agua Verde. When Señor Medina read Padre Ygnacio's letter and saw his brother's ring, he wept openly. He took me and Domingo into his arms, then we walked to the grand corridor and in front of his brother's portrait, he dropped to his knees.

"I didn't know," he whispered again and again. "My own flesh and blood and I didn't know. Forgive me, my brother. And forgive me, children."

Señora Medina was happy, too. She said that it was a sign from God. *"Dios provida,"* she said over and over. They plan on filing formal papers so that our last name legally becomes Medina. Señor Medina is so glad that his family name will not die out.

Rafaela and especially Gabriela squeezed me until I couldn't breathe. Gabriela jumped up and down and immediately begin giving me her dresses that no longer fit her growing body. She insisted I wear my hair in the latest style and put mother-of-pearl hair combs in the knot twisted on my head. She is happy to have me for a cousin, and I must admit I am proud to share her blood.

I am proud of your blood, too, Mamá. I vow that someday I will travel to the south where the last of your people live and seek out my grandfather and any other relatives left there.

Senor Medina explained to me and Domingo that our father owned land in the Sacramento Valley. The *mayordomo*, Villareal, had been secretly making a profit off it. But Señor Medina sent Villareal packing, and now the land is mine and Domingo's. Did you know that, Mamá? A small *rancho* occupies it now. Señor Medina and Gregorio took us there to see it. The hills — bright green from autumn rains — made my heart sing. Domingo saw wild horses in the meadow and became uncontrollable. He wants to round them up and brand them with a brand he has designed himself — the letter "M" with angel wings. Señor Medina laughed and tousled Domingo's hair. I think the señor is very glad that Domingo is his nephew. As for me, I can think of no better uncle on the face of the earth.

The *americanos* are coming more than ever now. Alta California is no more. The war goes badly for Mexico, and there is little hope that Santa Anna can defeat General Taylor's troops. It is just a matter of time until Mexico surrenders or is defeated. And what will become of Alta California? What will become of Rancho Agua Verde and all the *californios* who have made their homes here so long? I do not know. But our family will survive. Mamá, your blood and my father's blood will flow in the veins of California's children forever.

I am now fourteen, and Domingo is eleven. I found our birth dates in the records at Mission Dolores. We will move to the *rancho* as soon as I turn fifteen and am old enough to get married. I know exactly who I want to marry, if I can but make him see that we are perfect for each other. I promise that I will name my first daughter after you, Mamá. Thank you for sacrificing your life so that Domingo and I might live. I have saved every *peso* I can, and Señor Johnston has given me some money, too, for this headstone. With love, your daughter.

Mamá's headstone is small, but beautiful. It has an angel on one side and a rose vine on the other. The inscription says: CAROLINA MEDINA, 1810 – 1838. A LA PAZ DE DIOS.

Epilogue

❧❧

Rosalia continued living with the Johnstons for two more years, teaching Miguela how to cook and clean house. She did so not as a servant, but as a beloved cousin. Over the years they became the closest of friends.

In 1848, Rosalia and Domingo officially changed their last name to Medina and moved to their father's property in the Sacramento Valley. That same year, Johann Sutter told friends about the discovery of gold on a nearby river. As the word spread, thousands of Americans, Mexicans, South Americans, and Chinese flooded into Alta California searching for the precious yellow metal. Camps and boomtowns sprang up overnight. Henry Johnston seized the opportunity and made a fortune selling goods to the prospectors. He needed the money, for over the years Miguela bore eleven healthy children.

American squatters began settling on *rancho* lands belonging to the Medinas, General Vallejo, and other wealthy *californio* ranchers. They trampled crops, stole livestock, and pillaged homes. After California entered the Union in 1850, thousands of Americans claimed lands that had previously belonged to Mexican-Spanish families. The *rancheros* had to prove they owned the lands, and most of them lost fortunes paying for legal bills. Such was the case for Señor Medina. Penniless, he was forced to sell his land and moved to Monterey, where his married daughters, Rafaela and Gabriela, supported him and his wife.

Rosalia married Walter Johnston in 1851. Walter discovered a gold deposit in a creek on Rosalia's property. With her share of the gold money, Rosalia and Walter bought land in the Napa Valley. Walter tried his hand at raising grapevines imported from Germany. They grew wonderfully in the soil of the northern valleys. Soon he had a thriving business called Milagros Winery. Rosalia and Walter had five children, who all attended school and received good educations. She named her first two daughters Carolina and Nelly.

Domingo stayed on his inherited *rancho* and raised cattle and horses. He bred fighting bulls and fighting roosters. After the collapse of the Medina estate, Lupita and Gregorio came to live with him. Domingo married an Indian girl, an orphan whose people had become slave workers in the mines and fields.

Rosalia continued to keep a diary and even wrote poetry and fiction. One day, in the 1860s in Calaveras County, Rosalia chanced to meet a writer named Samuel Clemens. He told her she had great potential and encouraged her to submit her work to newspapers. Writing became part of Rosalia's life, and she published many stirring articles about bygone days at Rancho Agua Verde and the once sleepy little town of Yerba Buena, now renamed San Francisco.

In 1870, Rosalia had her father's remains brought to Mission Rafael and buried beside the woman he loved. She bought a new double headstone with entwining roses.

In 1906, at the age of seventy-three, while visiting the Johnstons, Rosalia was killed in the Great San Francisco Earthquake. She was buried next to her parents at Mission Rafael across the bay.

Glossary of Spanish Terms

adiós — good-bye

adobe — building material of sun-dried clay

agua verde — green water

alcalde — mayor of a town

a la paz de Dios — rest in peace with God

Alta California — Upper California

americano — American

anglo — an English-speaking person, especially one from the United States

arroyo — small streambed

Baja California — Lower California (a long, narrow peninsula)

banderilleros — men who stick small, colorful darts into the back of a bull during a bullfight

barranco — ravine, gully

bolero — a short, decorative jacket

buenas tardes — good afternoon

¡bueno! — good!

buñuelo — a sweet fried pastry

burro — a small, shaggy donkey

caballero — an expert horseman and gentleman of the upper class

cacique — an Indian word for "chief"

calaveras — an area where cattle are slaughtered for market, noted by piles of bones and skulls

californio — a Californian of Spanish ancestry

campo santo — Holy Ground; a cemetery next to a church

Candelaria — Candlemas, which occurs on February 2

cantina — a saloon

capote — a cape used by the matador to attract the charging bull

carreta — a cart with two large wheels, often pulled by oxen

casa grande — "great house"; the main house on a ranch estate

cascarónes — emptied eggshells filled with perfumed water or confetti

castillo — a tower to which intricate fireworks displays are attached

centavo — one hundredth of a peso; a penny

chile — pepper native to Central and South America

comal — a large, flat stone or clay dish on which tortillas are cooked

conquistadores — sixteenth-century Spaniards who conquered the native peoples of the New World by force

la corrida — a bullfight

curandero/a — a medicine man (or woman) who uses home remedies and rituals to heal

criollos — upper-class citizens born in Spanish America who were directly descended from Spaniards, with no Indian blood mixed in their ancestry

Día de los Muertos — Day of the Dead, a festival celebrated on All Souls' Day, November 2, to honor and remember deceased relatives. Images of death appear everywhere, as in Halloween

Dios provida — God will provide, a popular proverb

fandango — a Spanish dance; also, a party with dancing

fiesta — a festival, usually given to honor a religious occasion

gordita — a tortilla that is thicker than usual

gracias — thank you

¡Gracias a Dios! — thank goodness!

gran sala — a large room in the great house used mainly for entertaining

guitarra — guitar

hacienda — a large ranch estate in Mexico

herraderos — a big celebration held outdoors for the branding of the bulls

horno — an oven, often shaped like a beehive

indio — an Indian

José — Joseph

lazo — a lasso; a long braided rope with a special loop used for roping horses and cattle, typically rolled up and carried on the side of the saddle (see *la reata*)

loco — crazy

madre mía — mother mine, sometimes used as an expression of shock

mantilla — a delicate, decorative covering for a woman's head and face

manzanita — an evergreen shrub that bears small fruit

María — Mary

masa — dough prepared from a mixture of dried corn boiled in lime, then ground into a fine flour, which is used to make tamales and tortillas

matador — a bullfighter

mayordomo — an administrator for a large ranch or estate

mesteño — a mustang, a horse that runs with a wild herd

mestizo — a person who is half-Indian and half-Spanish

metate — a shallow, scooped-out stone onto which corn is ground into meal

milagro — a miracle

montera — a small black cap worn by the matador during a bullfight

muchacho — a boy

muy bonita — very pretty

Nochebuena — Christmas Eve

nopal — a prickly pear cactus

norteamericano — a citizen of the United States of North America

Osos — Bears; a nickname given to the Americans who declared California's independence from Mexico on June 14, 1846, because their flag had a bear drawn on it

padre — father; also the title of a priest, as in Padre Ygnacio

pan de los muertos — bread shaped like skulls, ghosts, or crossbones, baked for the Day of the Dead festival

pan dulce — sweet bread, a favorite dessert in Mexico

Pascua de Resurrección — Easter Sunday

pastorelas — lively plays in which the life of Jesus is portrayed

pepitas — pumpkin seeds, dried and made into a snack

pequito — very little

peso — Spanish silver coin, similar to a dollar

picadores — in a bullfight, men on horses who prick the bull to make it angry and weak before the matador enters the ring

piñata — a hollow clay container covered with papier-mâché of various shapes. At parties, children break the piñata open with a stick and scramble for the candy, nuts, and toys stuffed inside

plaza de toros — bullring

ponche — punch made from fruit juices

poncho — a blanket-like cloth with a hole cut in the center for the head to slip through

por favor — please

La Posada — a reenactment of the journey of Mary and Joseph looking for a place to stay in Bethlehem just before Jesus was born *presidio* — a military fort, especially one built near a mission in the New World

pueblo — small town

¿Qué pasa? — "What's going on?"

quinceanera — a girl's fifteenth birthday celebration, similar to a debutante ball

ramada — a shelter made from poles covered with branches; an arbor

ranchería — an Indian village or settlement

ranchero — a rancher

rancho — a large ranch, its primary business is the raising of livestock such as cattle and horses

la reata — a braided rawhide rope used to tie horses together (see *lazo*)

rebozo — a colorful blanketlike shawl worn by women around their shoulders

ristras — strings of tied-together vegetables, such as onions or red peppers

rodeo — a cattle roundup

sala — a parlor or drawing room; a family *sala* is similar to a den

sarape — a colorful blanket-like shawl worn around a man's shoulders

Semana Santa — Holy Week; the week immediately before Easter Sunday

Señor — sir, Mr.

Señora — madam, Mrs.

Señorita — Miss; a girl or unmarried woman

sí — yes

sierra — mountain range with jagged peaks, from Spanish word for saw

siesta — a rest taken after the midday meal, usually from 2:00 to 4:00 P.M.

¡Silencio! — Silence!

tamales — spiced pork covered in corn flour dough and cooked in corn husks

tortilla — a very thin circle made of corn flour and cooked on a grill

el toro — a bull

uno, dos, tres, cuatro, cinco — one, two, three, four, five

vaquero — a cowboy, a ranch hand who takes care of cattle

Vaya con Dios — Go with God, a greeting given when parting

veranda — a long, covered porch, often opening onto a courtyard

Yerba Buena — a small town on San Francisco Bay, later renamed San Francisco. Yerba Buena means "Good Herb."

LIFE IN AMERICA
IN 1846

HISTORICAL NOTE

In the 1530s, when Spanish explorers first spied a large landmass in the Pacific Ocean off the western shores of Mexico, they thought it was an island, and named the land "California," after a famous mythical island. In 1542, explorers discovered that California was not an island at all but a long, narrow peninsula attached to a great continent. They started calling the peninsula "Baja California" (Lower California) and the attached landmass "Alta California" (Upper California). Today Baja belongs to Mexico, while Alta California makes up the modern state of California.

The Spaniards found thousands of Native Americans living in Alta California, about 135 different peoples altogether, speaking about one hundred dialects. Natural barriers such as tall mountains to the east, uninhabitable desert to the south, and the Pacific Ocean to the west kept California Indians isolated from other native peoples of the Americas, giving them distinct cultures. Unlike the Indians of the

Great Plains who became expert horsemen and fiercely defended their way of life against American settlers in the 1800s, the California Indian tribes were smaller and relatively peaceful. They subsisted mainly by gathering nuts, berries, and roots and hunting fish and small game. These people flourished in the mild Pacific climate, and the population was estimated at three hundred thousand in the 1500s. Among the tribes were the Mojave, Miwok, Hupa, Pomo, Paiute, Yokuts, Maidu, Modoc, and Karok.

Ironically, Spanish explorers found no gold during their exploits, and Alta California remained uncolonized until 1769 when Franciscan padres, led by Father Junípero Serra, began establishing a line of Catholic missions from San Diego in the south to San Francisco Bay farther north. In addition to the missions where converted Indians worked and lived, Spain also built *presidios* — forts manned with soldiers and their families. *Pueblos* (small towns) sprang up nearby and attracted a few Spanish settlers who received land grants.

The missions flourished, successfully raising livestock and processing cattle products such as tallow and hides. These items were shipped to Mexico and created great revenues for the Church. But the price paid by the mission Indians was very high. They were hardly more than slaves, and many succumbed to the hard labor, crowded living conditions of missions, and European diseases against which they had no immunity. Epidemics often killed thousands at a time. By the time the missions started closing in 1834, over half of the native peoples had vanished.

In 1821, Mexico achieved independence from Spain and became a republic divided into states. Alta California became the most remote of the Mexican territories. The new government of Mexico began issuing land grants to settlers who moved to Alta California, including some foreigners. The Mexican government allowed Alta California residents to trade with foreign nations such as France, England, Russia, and the United States.

By 1834, the Mexican authorities began to disband the missions. Although the mission lands, livestock, vineyards, and orchards were supposed to be divided up among the mission Indians, in reality very little of the land actually ended up in the hands of the Native Americans. Most of the mission lands and livestock was given to descendants of Spanish settlers in the area and to newly arrived, upper-class Mexican settlers. These grants were very large — thousands of acres —

and grand cattle *ranchos* sprang up. The *rancheros*, especially those in southern Alta California, grew very successful and wealthy, ushering in the famous days of luxurious country life, accentuated with parties, *fiestas*, and bullfights. Some *rancheros* became so wealthy by raising cattle that they eventually stopped manufacturing their own goods. They came to depend on trade from other nations for furniture, cloth, tools, weapons, and even leather products such as shoes or saddles. Former mission Indians and *mestizos* (half-Indian, half-Spanish) worked on the *ranchos* as *vaqueros* (cowboys), field laborers, or house servants.

Only a few Americans, mostly sailors on merchant ships, had visited Alta California. But in 1826, Jedediah Smith led the first overland Americans, a group of trappers. They found Alta California a fur paradise, and the word spread of its abundant game and fertile lands. In 1841, John Bidwell led the first successful wagon train of Americans across the Great Plains, over the Sierra Nevada, and into Alta California's fertile green valleys. These Americans received grants from the Mexican government to settle in California and had to agree to become Mexican citizens, become Catholics, learn to speak Spanish, and obey the laws of Mexico.

One of the earliest foreign settlers was a Swiss immigrant named Johann Augustus Sutter, who received a land grant near the convergence of the Sacramento and American Rivers. Sutter established a settlement named "New Helvetia," which included a fort, orchards, vineyards, fields of grains, and many craftsmen. Sutter's Fort became a favorite stopping place for American settlers coming by wagon train over the Sierra Nevada mountains. The settlement also included trappers, hunters, and former sailors.

The distance between Alta California and the capital of Mexico City made rule a difficult matter. The Spanish-speaking citizens of Alta California called themselves *californios*. Proud and independent-minded, they considered themselves Californians first and Mexicans second. They learned that they could not depend on Mother Mexico to supply soldiers for protection, money for settlements, or wise government officials. Governors sent to Alta California by Mexico City always fared poorly and were often driven away. This fierce independent nature kept Alta California in a state of constant political turmoil, in which factions in the north fought with factions in the south for control.

Between 1841 and 1845, about two thousand

American settlers arrived in Alta California. Some "squatted" on *ranchero* lands or entered illegally without receiving proper grants from the Mexican government. In 1845, Captain John Frémont, an American army engineer, led a party of sixty men into California, claiming he was surveying the mountain passes for the wagon trains. The local *californios* became suspicious of the motives of the Americans. They well remembered what had happened with Texas in 1836.

Tension between Mexico and the United States had been increasing since 1836, when Texas declared its independence from Mexico. Mexico did not recognize the treaty signed by General Antonio Santa Anna and still claimed Texas. In December 1845, Texas was annexed by the United States, sparking the Mexican-American War. General Zachary Taylor and one hundred thousand men crossed the Rio Grande into Mexico, and the first of many bloody battles began.

Alta California, isolated and always late to receive news, did not know the war had begun in Mexico. On June 14, 1846, a small band of American trappers led by William B. Ide took up arms against the acknowledged leader of northern Alta California, General Mariano Vallejo, who resided in Sonoma. They placed him under arrest and declared California to be the free and independent Republic of California. Their makeshift flag included a grizzly bear, thus giving their declaration the nickname of "the Bear Flag Revolt."

The Republic of California was short-lived. By July 7, American warships arrived in Monterey, the military capital, and took Alta California for the United States without a battle. In northern California, the residents accepted American rule with little resistance, but in southern California, the *californios* fought gallantly and defeated the Americans in several battles. Their last victory occurred at the Battle of San Pascual on December 6, 1846. But their efforts came too late. In several bloody battles in central Mexico, General Santa Anna's forces were defeated, and a peace agreement was signed in 1847. In the final Treaty of Guadalupe-Hidalgo, Mexico sold all her northern provinces, including what became New Mexico, Arizona, Nevada, and California to the United States.

Life in California might have resumed to normal were it not for the fact that in 1847, while building a mill, one of Johann Sutter's men discovered gold. At first the word reached only locals. Overnight, California towns emptied as men left for the goldfields to make a fortune. As word spread south and west across the Pacific Ocean, experienced miners came from Mexico, South America, China, and Hawaii.

Americans on the East Coast, however, did not receive the news until December 1848, when President James K. Polk officially announced the gold strike in California. This triggered a flood of American "forty-niners" the next year. The population of California increased from a few thousand to over one hundred thousand in just one year. Because of a lack of supplies, prices skyrocketed. Many entrepreneurs made fortunes selling goods to the miners, and *rancheros* made fortunes selling beef. The tiny port town once called Yerba Buena was renamed San Francisco, and became the main stopping point for gold-seekers arriving by sea.

California became the thirty-first state in the Union in 1850. The gold rush increased awareness of California's isolation. To get there by sea or by overland wagon train took months of grueling, often dangerous travel. It was obvious that California needed to be connected to the rest of the United States. By the mid-1860s, the great railroad race began, with the Central Pacific line running east from California, and the Union Pacific line running west from Missouri.

Most of the work for the Central Pacific was done by Chinese immigrants who endured harsh, dangerous conditions and discrimination. The two lines met at Promontory Summit, Utah, on May 10, 1869, uniting the nation and ending California's longtime isolation.

By the turn of the century the gold rush was long over. Most of the Native Americans of California had vanished, and their lifestyles were forgotten. Many of the wealthy *californio* ranchers lost their holdings in land disputes over the years or went bankrupt paying legal fees. As the American population grew, the Spanish-speaking *californios* found themselves in the minority and lost political influence. The grand life on the *rancheros* became a thing of the past, but Spanish influence remains a deep-seated part of California culture.

This detail (also pictured on the cover) depicts Rosa, the Indian saint after whom the northern California town of Santa Rosa was named. Although she graces the cover, this book is in no way based on her.

The process of settling Alta California was accelerated when Spain established a string of Catholic missions along the coastline. They provided food, clothing, and religious instruction to the indigenous population, but the regime was often harsh. Many Indians died from the hard labor or from European diseases. By the mid-1800s, the native peoples had vanished as a society. This is a detail of an etching that shows mission life at Santa Cruz in the days when the founding padres resided there.

Chores were the most important part of everyday life for servants in Alta California as all food and clothing was made from scratch. Here, a cook at a California rancho grinds corn kernels between a heavy stone roller and a slab.

Tasks like doing the washing became all day events that were at once tiresome and fun outings for everyone involved. Large groups would travel to Agua Caliente, Hot Spring, in the early dawn, spending the day in the water, washing loads and loads of laundry, and enjoying the day-long "vacation" from rancho chores.

El Día de los Muertos, *The Day of the Dead,* is an ancient Mexican festival that originated with the Aztecs and paid homage to the dead. Catholic Spaniards revised the festival to coincide with All Souls' Day. Today it is celebrated with parades, parties, visits to the graves of deceased relatives, and special pastries such as pan de los muertos, *bread of the dead.*

Ranchos were often the site of lavish parties, or fiestas. Sometimes the preparations for such grand celebrations as weddings took weeks or even months. Women dressed in their most beautiful clothes, with colorful skirts and lace hair decorations. Traditional dances like the fandango, along with music and everyone's favorite foods, made for very memorable parties indeed.

211

Bullfighting, an integral part of Spanish culture, came north to California with the Mexicans. The bullfight, along with all of its ritual glamour, was an event to behold, complete with handsomely dressed matadors poised to dance the graceful prelude to the main event—the defeat of the ill-fated opponent.

General Mariano Guadalupe Vallejo (1808–1890) turned Sonoma from a mission town into a Mexican pueblo, built around a beautiful eight-acre central plaza (still the largest in California) that survives today as the center of city life and has been named a national monument. He laid out the plaza and the street grid, and made Sonoma, briefly, the center of traffic and trade north of San Francisco. He also gave it the Indian name "Valley of the Moon." Vallejo gained enormous property holdings, wealth, and power. He was named military governor of the state in 1836 and controlled much of northern California.

212

Pastelitos de Boda
(Wedding Cookies)

Ingredients:

$^1/_2$ cup of butter (1 stick), softened

1 cup powdered sugar

2 cups flour

1 cup finely chopped pecans

2 tsp. vanilla extract

$^1/_2$ cup powdered sugar to roll cookies in

1) Preheat oven to 350°. Butter or grease baking sheets.

2) In large mixing bowl combine first five ingredients.

3) Stir until dough forms. Roll dough into 1-inch balls.

4) Place balls on buttered baking sheets.

5) Bake for 10 minutes (or until cookies are lightly browned). Using hot pads, remove from oven. Cool slightly, then remove from baking sheets using spatula.

6) Place $^1/_2$ cup powdered sugar in large bowl or on a plate. While the baked cookies are still warm, roll them in the powdered sugar until completely covered.

Makes about 3 dozen cookies

Cielito Lindo
(Lovely Heaven)

De la Sierra Morena,
Cielito lindo, viene bajando.
Un par de ojitos negros
Cielito lindo de contrabando

Ay, ay, ay, ay.
Canta y no llores.
Porqué cantando se alegran
Cielito lindo los corazones.

Un flecha en el aire,
Cielito lindo, lanzó cupido,
Y ese flecha volando
Cielito lindo, bien me ha herido.

Ay, ay, ay, ay.
Canta y no llores.
Porqué cantando se alegran
Cielito lindo los corazones.

This is a love song that a young man sings to his girlfriend. He calls her his "cielito lindo."
She has beautiful black eyes and she comes down the Sierra Morena mountain to see him.
The chorus of the song says: "Sing, don't cry," because singing makes one's heart happy.

American settlers pouring into California over the Sierras challenged Mexican power in the 1840s. Mexican rule ended in 1846 with the Bear Flag Revolt. The revolt started in Sonoma when this flag was raised on June 14. In 1848, Mexico was forced to cede all of Alta California and the rest of the Southwest to the United States.

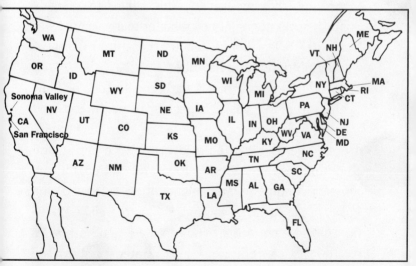

This modern map of the United States shows the approximate locations of the Sonoma Valley and San Francisco.

About the Author

"My interest in the Mexican culture began early. I was born in the Rio Grande valley of Texas on the U.S.-Mexican border. I was surrounded by the sights and sounds of Mexico, from the lyrical Spanish language of the workers in orange groves near our house to the music coming from open windows. I soaked up the language, the culture, the spirit of the people during those early years. As an adult, I lived in a largely Spanish-speaking neighborhood for many years. I was fortunate to learn more about the culture through wonderful friends and neighbors.

I have been fascinated with the history of New Spain for many years, especially how Indian and Spanish ways blended to create the Mexican culture. To me, the Mexican culture is one of contrast and compromise, one of both love and hatred for the Spanish conquerors and missionaries. When writing *Valley of the Moon*, I wanted to create a girl who reflected these contrasts, who represesented both sides of the Mexican culture. I also wanted to show the richness of California's Spanish-Mexican history and how the events of the Bear Flag Revolt changed the lives of the Spanish-speaking *californios*, and ultimately the history of the United States."

Sherry Garland is the critically acclaimed author of twenty-five books for children, young adults, and adults, including one previous Dear America title, *A Line in the Sand: The Alamo Diary of Lucinda Lawrence*. Her picture books have won honors such as ALA Notable and Reading Rainbow Selection. Her YA books have been named ALA Best Books for Young Adults, Best Books for Reluctant Readers, and the American Booksellers' "Pick of the Lists," and have also appeared on the New York Public Library's "Best Books for the Teen Age." She is also the recipient of the California Reader's Choice Award, the Texas Institute of Letters Award, and the Lamplighter Award. Her recent Scholastic title, *My Father's Boat*, was named a CBC Notable Trade Book in the field of Social Sciences. She lives in central Texas with her husband.

ACKNOWLEDGMENTS

I am greatly indebted to Eric Stanley, Director of Education at the Sonoma County Museum, for generously reading my manuscript for historical accuracy and for making helpful suggestions. Deepest appreciation also goes to Beth Levine for her editing, to Diane Garvey Nesin for her tedious fact-checking, to Zoe Moffitt for the photo research, and to Cristina Costantino for the beautiful cover design. Thanks also go to Tracy Mack for originally suggesting this topic and to Amy Griffin for her editorial support.

Cover portrait and page 209 (top): Detail of *Rosa*, 1924, painted by Grace Carpenter Hudson, from the collection of Nancy and David Berto.

Cover background and page 209 (bottom): Detail of *Mission Nuestra Señora de la Soledad*, painting by Oriana Day, late nineteenth century, Fine Arts Museums of San Francisco, gift of Mrs. Eleanor Martin, DY37565.

Page 210 (top): Woman grinding corn for tortillas, Seaver Center for Western History Research, Natural History Museum of Los Angeles County.

Page 210 (bottom): Washing day, from *Sketches of Early California: A Collection of Personal Adventures*. Introduction and Commentaries by Oscar Lewis. Compiled by Donald DeNevi. Chronicle Books, San Francisco, 1971.

Page 211 (top): *Day of the Dead* ©2001 Banco de México, Diego Rivera & Frida Kahlo Museums Trust Av. Cinco de Mayo No. 2, Col. Del. Cuauhtémoc 06059, México D.F., Archivo CENIDIAP/INBA, Centro de las Artes, Biblioteca de las Artes (México).

Page 211 (bottom): Fiesta scene, Henry Groskinsky. Courtesy of Mr. and Mrs. W. Edwin Gledhill.

Page 212 (top): Bullfight arena, oil on canvas, 1833, by Johann Moritz Rugendas, The Granger Collection, New York.

Page 212 (bottom): General Vallejo, Sonoma County Library and Petaluma Library.

Page 215 (top): The Bear Flag of the California Republic being raised at Sonoma: mural by Anton Refregier, The Granger Collection, New York.

West to a Land of Plenty
The Diary of Teresa Angelino Viscardi
by Jim Murphy

Dreams in the Golden Country
The Diary of Zipporah Feldman
by Kathryn Lasky

A Line in the Sand
The Alamo Diary of Lucinda Lawrence
by Sherry Garland

Standing in the Light
The Captive Diary of Catherine Carey Logan
by Mary Pope Osborne

Voyage on the Great *Titanic*
The Diary of Margaret Ann Brady
by Ellen Emerson White

My Heart Is on the Ground
The Diary of Nannie Little Rose, a Sioux girl
by Ann Rinaldi

The Great Railroad Race
The Diary of Libby West
by Kristiana Gregory

The Girl Who Chased Away Sorrow
The Diary of Sarah Nita, a Navajo Girl
by Ann Turner

A Light in the Storm
The Civil War Diary of Amelia Martin
by Karen Hesse

A Coal Miner's Bride
The Diary of Anetka Kaminska
by Susan Campbell Bartoletti

Color Me Dark
The Diary of Nellie Lee Love
by Patricia McKissack

One Eye Laughing, the Other Weeping
The Diary of Julie Weiss
by Barry Denenberg

My Secret War
The World War II Diary of Madeline Beck
by Mary Pope Osborne

Seeds of Hope
The Gold Rush Diary of Susanna Fairchild
by Kristiana Gregory

For Tony and Lydia Garcia,
muchas gracias, amigos.

❧ ❧

**While the events described and some of the characters
in this book may be based on actual historical events
and real people, María Rosalia de Milagros is a fictional character,
created by the author, and her journal and its epilogue
are works of fiction.**

Copyright © 2001 by Sherry Garland

❧ ❧

All rights reserved. Published by Scholastic Inc.
DEAR AMERICA, SCHOLASTIC, and associated logos are trademarks
and/or registered trademarks of Scholastic Inc.

Library of Congress Cataloging-in-Publication Data
Garland, Sherry.
Valley of the Moon : the diary of Maria Rosalia de Milagros /
by Sherry Garland.
p. cm. - (Dear America)
Summary: The 1845-1846 diary of thirteen-year-old Maria, servant
to the wealthy Spanish family which took her in when her Indian
mother died. Includes a historical note about the settlement and early
history of California.
ISBN (paper over board) 0-439-08820-8
1. California - History - 1846-1850 - Juvenile fiction. [1. California -
History - 1846-1850 - Fiction. 2. Household employees - Fiction.
3. Racially mixed people - Fiction. 4. Orphans - Fiction.
5. Diaries - Fiction.] I. Title. II. Series.
PZ7.G18415 Val 2001
[Fic] - dc21   00-055620
CIP

10 9 8 7 6 5 4 3 2 1   01 02 03 04 05

The text type was set in Goudy.
The display type was set in Herculanum.
Book design by Elizabeth B. Parisi
Photo research by Zoe Moffit

Printed in the U.S.A.   23
First edition, April 2001

❧ ❧